REVOLUTION
CHRONICLES OF THE UPRISING: 3

K.A. Salidas

Revolution
ISBN 978-0-9851277-9-4
Copyright © 2014 by K.A. Salidas

Cover Layout by Willsin Rowe http://willsinrowe.blogspot.com/
Interior Layout by Katie Salidas http://www.katiesalidas.com
Editing by Sharazade http://sharazade.com/?p=825

Published by:
Rising Sign Books
http://www.risingsignbooks.net

For more information about my books email:
katiesalidas@gmail.com

CHRONICLES OF THE UPRISING

Dissension - The great cataclysm wiped almost all life from the face of planet Earth, but tiny pockets of survivors crawled from the ashes, with only one thought: survival, at any cost.

But not all survivors were human.

In the dark, military society that has risen in the aftermath, vampires, once thought to be mythical, have been assimilated and enslaved. Used for blood sport their lives are allowed to continue only for the entertainment of the masses. Reviled as savages, they are destined to serve out their immortal lives in the arena, as gladiators.

And there is no greater gladiator than Mira: undefeated, uncompromising...and seemingly unbreakable. When an escape attempt leads Mira into the path of Lucian Stavros, the city's Regent, her destiny is changed forever.

Lucian, raised in a culture which both reviles and celebrates the savagery and inhumanity of vampires, finds Mira as intriguing as she is brash. An impulsive decision - to become Mira's patron – changes more than just Lucian's perception about vampire kind. The course of his life is altered in ways he could never have predicted – a life that is suddenly as expendable as hers.

Can Mira prove to Lucian that all is not as it seems? Can Lucian escape centuries of lies, bloodshed, and propaganda to see the truth? Or will the supreme power of the human overlords destroy them both?

Complication - Narrowly escaping death at the hands of the Magistrate, Mira travels west, toward the coast. With three weakened human fugitives accompanying her, she searches for the mythical land of Sanctuary.

After encountering a pack of wolf shifters, headed by the charismatic—and brazen—Stryker, Mira learns that Sanctuary is real after all. Caldera Grove: home of the Otherkin. Hidden in the mouth of a dormant volcano, it has protected its residents from humans since the early days following the great cataclysm. For Mira— a vampire— Caldera Grove is a land of peace; an escape from the relentless persecution of the humans who once enslaved her, and an end to the daily struggle and bloodshed of being a gladiator.

For the humans accompanying her, Caldera Grove means death. Humans, greedy and untrustworthy creatures, are destroyed before they can penetrate its borders.

To plead her case for entry into Caldera, Mira must abandon her companions, albeit temporarily, and follow Stryker into the heart of the city. What she finds within Caldera Grove presents her with an unenviable decision between her own desires for freedom and peace, or honor and the human companions who risked it all for her.

Revolution - Peace is an illusion. Blood, violence, and death follow Mira like shadows.

Battle lines have been drawn between human and Otherkin, and a bloody war is on the horizon: one that will end in either a shift in the world's balance of power...or ultimate destruction.

In spite of their strength, powers, and a rage known only by the oppressed, the Otherkin are evenly matched by the superior numbers of the human army. To tip the balance in their favor, the Otherkin need more soldiers – and their only options are the Gladiators of New Haven city.

Mira is sent across enemy lines to recruit any able-bodied vampires to her cause. But what she discovers along the way will blur the lines between friends and enemies. Seeds of doubt weaken Mira's allegiance, and she finds herself torn between the old masters who used her as entertainment and the new ones who consider her as nothing more than a weapon.

As the war draws near, Mira will have to decide what she is truly fighting for.

Transition - Peace is just a breath between battles for Mira. Hardened by slavery and war, she longs for the simpler life, knowing that it might never be hers to enjoy. There is always another battle waiting to be fought, another foe on the horizon. Peace between humans, vampires, and otherkin may be nothing more than a dream, but Mira holds out hope. It is during this brief respite that Mira is gifted one of her greatest weapons. Though it brings with it memories of a time when she was not so jaded, it also comes with a reminder of terrible pain and loss. Awakening deeply hidden emotions within her, if Mira can use this to her advantage, she'll have a new ally in the next battle to come.

More Titles planned. For more information visit www.KatieSalidas.com

CHAPTER ONE

Silvery moonlight bled through the sheer curtains above Mira's head. Cradled in the warmth of the pillowy mattress, Mira could have stayed in bed for all eternity. She could hardly remember a time when she'd been so comfortable. Thirty years in a dirty cell had made her forget the simple comforts of a warm bed and soft clothes. The breeze drifted in, picking up the curtains and sending them lazily dancing. She reached up, letting them tickle her fingertips, and noticed something she'd ever seen before. Well, at least something she hadn't seen in a very long time. Her hands were clean. Truly clean… and soft. No caked-on blood and grime, or gunk embedded into her nail beds. They even smelled of lemongrass and sandalwood, and were smoother than she'd ever known, thanks to the oils and lotions Stryker had provided her. This was how things were supposed to be. Life was not supposed to be dirty and ugly. Life was meant to be lived, and small comforts like this enjoyed, not ended by the swift stroke of her sword at the order of her masters. Though she missed the comfortable weight of her weapon, she'd gladly give it up if it meant never having to fight again.

She sighed contentedly and let the squishy mattress hug every inch of her body. This was heaven.

If she could somehow stop time, make the moment last forever, she would. Not being a very devout vampire, Mira still silently prayed – begged really – to the gods for more of this blissful peace. Hope kept the dream alive, but Mira knew the truth. This was only a brief peaceful interlude, one she so desperately needed, but it would be short-lived.

Mira was a warrior. Fighting was her life, try as she might to deny it, and the looming dread of what was to come weighed heavily on her heart.

She should have been up and moving, sunset having long since passed, but she couldn't tear her eyes away from the window. So many evenings lost. So many missed opportunities to take in the breathtaking majesty of the starlit sky. Thirty years of imprisonment deep underground had robbed her of everything she'd once taken for granted, and now that she was finally able to see and appreciate the twinkling stars, Mira wasn't wasting one second of it.

In less than forty-eight hours, she'd be back on the road to almost certain death.

She pulled a soft knit blanket up to her shoulders to ward off the slight chill in the air.

Everything comes with a price. Caldera Grove. Beautiful, mystical, and earthy, it promised that longed-for freedom to Mira, and a life free of prejudice. But that did not extend to the humans who'd accompanied her. Lucian, Sarah, and Curtis's fate depended on Mira. She'd already paid dearly in the struggle for her own freedom, but it had not been enough to ensure her friends' safety. The price promised to cost her more than she would be able to pay… a trip back to New Haven, behind the Iron Gate.

Hardened warrior as she was, thinking of returning to that dreadful place made her cringe. Silver-coated bars. UV torches. The lightbox. Thirty years spent trying to escape from within those walls. Enduring unbearable tortures and being forced to kill for the entertainment of her masters.

Anger turned to bile in the back of her throat, threatening to sour the peaceful moment she'd been enjoying.

It was best not to think of such things. Live in the moment. Enjoy the comfort. Savor the delectably squishy mattress at her back, and the chilly breeze blowing in. These luxuries deserved to be cherished.

"Mira, are you up?" Lucian's voice, muffled slightly, penetrated the thick wooden door of the room she was using for sleep. "We're scheduled to meet with the Council."

The root of her latest set of problems. The Otherkin Council. Mira grumbled, "Bunch of pompous asses. Self-absorbed and out of touch..." Other choice descriptions came to mind, but name-calling wasn't going to change the fact that she owed them a debt that had to be paid. And she had to at least make the effort to play nicely until she left the walls of Caldera Grove. She was just as much on their good side as they were hers. But, it was by their good graces she and the humans had been allowed within the boundaries of Caldera Grove, and she had to cooperate, much as it annoyed her to do so.

Lucian must not have heard her grumbling. He knocked on the door and waited a moment before saying, "Mira? Can I come in?"

She wanted to say no. His very presence reminded her of the duty she must perform, and all she wanted to do at that moment was forget her troubles. Heaving a heavy sigh, Mira reluctantly tossed aside her blanket and stood. "Yeah, get in here!"

Lucian pushed the door open but did not step inside. "Making yourself at home, I see." His mossy eyes spoke more than words about his discomfort and deep-rooted anger.

"Shouldn't I be as comfortable as possible while I can?" Damn his silent judgment of her. She deserved a little rest and recuperation after all she'd been through. "It's not often I get to enjoy such luxury."

She could see the words forming, but Lucian did not speak them. Nothing about this place was luxurious to him, nor was he happy with their situation.

"Have you been mistreated?" she asked, wondering if she'd missed something beyond their hosts' prejudice.

"Quite the contrary." Lucian folded his arms and leaned against the doorframe. His posture might have looked relaxed, but she saw past the ruse to the Elite within him, rising to the surface. The pampered prince throwing a temper tantrum, but desperately trying to hide it. "Stryker's pack has been quite congenial. But we're quarantined here. Only allowed to leave with your escort. I'd have loved to explore the city."

"You will in time." Mira tried to hold back the smirk. Thirty years she'd been imprisoned in a tiny cell, and he was daring to complain to her about having to stay inside the wolf-pack's large den all day? In some ways, though she dare not admit it out loud, she felt a little vindication seeing Lucian's discomfort. After all, he had enjoyed his Elite status and all that entailed while she'd spent all those years as a gladiator.

"Yes, of course. I'll be able to explore after the suicide mission." Sarcasm made him sound petulant, but she decided best not to call him out on it yet. "Assuming, that is, I make it back in one piece. Speaking of that, we should head to our meeting about our impending death. The Council is waiting."

"Don't sound so positive, Lucian. People will think we've swapped bodies."

His eyes narrowed slightly, forming tiny creases at the corners. "Are you not bothered by the fact we are going to die?"

Mira shook her head. Death threats had been her way of life for so long they'd become white noise. Of course she was not ready to die, but there was no point in acknowledging those fears. "Everyone dies eventually. Enjoy the ride and make the trip worthwhile."

"Spoken like someone ready to die." His tone fell flat, as If he'd already accepted defeat and the inevitable.

As much as she owed him her allegiance, his mood swings were testing the limits of her patience. "I can see you're stressed, so I'll forgive the temper tantrum this time… Suck it up, Elite."

Her use of that word had the intended effect, rendering Lucian speechless. Jaw hanging wide, he looked positively stunned. Behind his eyes she saw a multitude of emotions fighting to surface. She stared him down, daring him to say something else stupid and give her a reason to shut him up. He was better than this. She knew it. This moodiness had to stop, one way or another.

After the moment had passed, and he appeared to have calmed, Mira spoke again. "Will Sarah and Curtis be joining us?"

"They're required to attend." Though much calmer now, contempt still tainted his voice. "Escorted guard and all."

"You're going to have to drop the attitude. The tables have turned. You're no Elite here. You are nothing to them… until you show them your worth."

Lucian let out a sigh. His shoulders slumped. "You're right. I'm being an arrogant idiot about all of this."

"Remember, those are your words, not mine." Though she whole-heartedly agreed with them.

"These last few days have been so trying."

Mira closed the gap between them. Her first thought was to reach out and comfort him, but stopped herself. Touching was what other people did, hugging and hand holding. She could try to emulate it, give the pouting human what he wanted. But unnecessary touching felt odd and mechanical. Physical contact wasn't what he needed anyway. A swift kick in the ego would do. "I'm trying my best not to laugh now."

Her snarky comment earned a much more acceptable impish smile from the human. "Laughing at my misfortune; how very magnanimous of you." Lucian crossed his arms, making him look even more the pouting child.

"Not sure what that word means, but sure. I've been tortured and damn near killed. Risked my life and put my neck on the line for you... and you're grumpy."

"And pouting like a little child. Yes. I hear you loud and clear. I'll shut up now."

"Finally." She winked. "We're on the same page."

"I'm just not used to this. Not that it should be an excuse, I know. I'll suck it up, as you said, and try harder to be accepting of their ... hospitability."

"I wouldn't go as far as calling them hospitable just yet. They're only harboring you until the outcome of the suicide mission."

Finally, his mood truly lifted, and Lucian even let slip a laugh. "I love how blunt you are, Mira."

"Pussy-footing doesn't get you anywhere. And neither does procrastination. Let's get moving." She grabbed a light shawl from a hanger by the door and threw it over her shoulders. The air in Caldera was chillier than she was used to, and though she enjoyed it, Mira was finding it left her cold to the bones after only a short while. Blame slow vampire circulation for that, but at least there were warm clothes to compensate.

The wolves' den was surprisingly quiet at this early hour of the night. Their room was one of many off the great circular shaped living space. Even to her enhanced hearing, there were hardly any sounds of life in the building. Two figures, human by the smell of them, were lounging by the fire, but aside from that, the place was empty. Odd, she thought. Mira would have expected to see at least some of the pack milling about in the great room. They had, after all, been told they had to have an escort anywhere they went. Why leave them alone, then? Questions for another time.

Mira headed for the door, expecting a guard to be placed there, but again found nothing. Not that they could go far on their own; Caldera was far from a huge city, and they were obviously newcomers. On orders to stay put until an escort came for them, any misstep would certainly be reported. *Oh, well.* She'd deal with the repercussions if any arose; they were meant to go visit the Council anyway. She opened the door, intending to walk there herself, when Stryker rounded the corner at the end of the street. He spotted her and waved.

As escorts went, he was certainly preferable. She knew he was on her side of things. And not too bad in a fight, either. She waved back and waited for him to make it to the door.

Fresh from a run, he had the scent of sweat on his skin, but Mira secretly felt a pang of disappointment that he was clothed instead of in his usual natural state. Shifters did not seem to mind nudity, and neither did Mira. A well-toned body was always a sight to appreciate.

"Drooling again, Mira?" Stryker flashed her a toothy grin as he brushed past her in the doorway. She purposely stood her ground so they would touch and she could get a deeper breath of his manly scent before it was gone.

Lucian crossed his arms, setting his mouth into a hard line. Not sure if his aggressive stare was directed at Mira or Stryker, she shrugged it off and licked her fangs. "Hungry, actually."

"Wild for more wolf, eh?" Stryker's amber eyes sparkled at her.

That got a rise out of Lucian. The air of Elite decorum fell as he practically snarled, "You fed from him?"

"Yeah, why?" Confused by his appalled tone, Mira stepped back from both men.

Eyes cast down to the ground with uncharacteristic abashment, Lucian quietly mumbled, "Nothing. I forget your nature sometimes."

There was more behind his words, but Mira had neither the time nor the desire to drag it out of him. She was a vampire. She was free. She could feed on whomever she pleased.

Unfazed by either her comments or Lucian's grimacing face, Stryker walked passed Mira into the house. "Let me change, and I'll escort you to the meeting. You can stop by the clinic if you need to, Mira. There should be donors available."

"I can wait until we've finished our meeting. As I understand it, we've inconvenienced the Council enough."

"Don't pretend you care," Stryker laughed. He disappeared behind a door. Mira could hear him moving about in the room.

Lucian stood awkwardly silent for a few moments before he finally spoke. "I'll go speak with Sarah and Curtis until we are ready to leave." He turned away from Mira and walked toward another set of doors off the circular main room.

"We're here." Curtis lifted a hand and waved at his leader. He and his wife sat snuggled up together in a large cushioned seat near the fire. "Just waiting on you, sir."

Lucian walked passed, brushing Mira's shoulder roughly with his own as he headed toward the fire. Passive aggressive was not becoming on him, though she read the message loud and clear: he was disappointed with her, but for what reason, she couldn't fathom. Humans were so touchy about things at times.

Stryker reemerged from his room dressed in linen pants and a long tunic belted at the waist, similar to what she'd been outfitted in when she was a gladiator. It struck her as odd to see someone from this place dressed like a slave. "Do you think I'll pass for one of your prisoners?"

The question was directed at Lucian, but Stryker looked almost excitedly at Mira.

She shrugged, trying not to let the anguish she felt remembering her time in the prison rise to the surface. "Looks too clean."

"We'll dirty it up on the way, then." Stryker closed the gap between himself and Mira. "If we can utilize the element of surprise…"

"I see where you're going with this, but slaves are imprisoned when they are not fighting. You'd never find one roaming the halls, and certainly not without guard."

"Details I've considered. I have the uniforms from the soldiers we felled on our journey."

His attention to detail impressed Mira. A warrior with a sharp mind too. No wonder he was an Alpha. She was glad she had him on her side. He had already proved to be so helpful and would continue to be so. "You surprise me, wolf."

"I'll take that as a compliment, vampire." He winked and flashed her a devilish grin. She loved their little jabs, the playful to and fro between them. Stryker was so easy to get along with.

"I'll take you all now to the Council chambers." Stryker waved his hand directing everyone out of the house.

CHAPTER TWO

They walked along the moonlit roads toward the center of Caldera, Stryker and Mira taking the lead with the humans close behind. Though she'd seen it all before on her previous visit, Mira couldn't help but slow her pace so she could properly take in the sights and smells of this paradise for the supernatural. Only a short while ago, this place had been all but myth to her, and now she was *this close* to calling it her home.

Knowing it was folly, she dared to dream that one day it just might be the place she called home. Suicide mission or not.

Middle of the night as it was, the city was alive and vital. Vampires, shifters, and Otherkin alike were busy with the hustle and bustle of their nightly activities. Small shop owners with their doors wide open to the night air waved and smiled, inviting Mira's small group inside for a peek at their wares. Although she was tempted, Mira didn't stray from her path. But she did promise herself plenty of time for exploration when they came back victorious. She smiled and waved back at those who were courteous to her. Being a prisoner had not stripped her of manners, though some might have thought that was the case.

Not all passersby looked on Mira's group with friendly eyes, however. She noticed more than one wayward glance or suspicious glare from residents of the city. She expected as much for her companions – humans, after all – but not to her from her own kind. Their visible anger made Mira feel ill at ease. The Council was already breathing down her throat; she had not considered having to win over the city inhabitants too. The hope of peace, the small spark she'd been holding onto so fiercely, suddenly dimmed.

"They know you brought the humans," Stryker answered her unasked question, thankfully without a hint of anger or condescension in his voice. "You'd be hard-pressed to find any popularity right now."

Mira shrugged, hoping to hide the worry she felt rising to the surface. "I don't need popularity, just acceptance." In truth, she needed both. Not necessarily popularity in the traditional sense, but kinship, companionship – people like her who valued her. Being a slave for so long and having her only value be the amount of wins she'd racked up had skewed her sense of self-worth. Deep down she longed for someone to like her for something beyond her ability to rip a throat out.

"Acceptance you can have easily enough. You're one of us. But them…" Stryker cocked his head sideways and glanced back at the human trio following behind. "They'll probably never find acceptance here as long as they remain human."

Still pushing for her to turn them, even after she'd put her foot down. Would he ever stop? "I still think that's petty. Just for the record."

Now it was Stryker's turn to shrug, but he wasn't doing it to hide anything, Mira knew he didn't care one way or the other. "It is what it is. We just have to deal with it."

"Maybe not. We're going on a suicide mission, remember?"

"Always the optimist, aren't we?"

"Realist. How many times do I have to say it?"

"Well, realistically, we do stand a chance. We just need a good plan to get in and get your vampires released. I'm quite certain they can take care of the nitty gritty parts of continuing their freedom."

"Delicately put," Mira snickered. *Why must everyone pussyfoot around the topic of drinking blood?*

"I do try. Maybe you should too." His smile went far beyond playful, but the message was as serious as the grave.

"Is that your nice way of telling me to shut up and let others do the talking?" Her mouth had always been a problem. And though she hated to be reminded of that fact, she knew there was truth there. She often let it run wild, and this was not the time for it. At least Stryker was trying to tell her nicely; that was more courtesy than she'd been given in more years than she could count.

"No. Don't shut up. Your input is valid… just maybe try not to piss anyone off with it. Filter your words. We're trying to be on the same team here."

"You and my friends back there are on the same team. But… the Council… I have my doubts."

"They have the best interests of our people at heart, as hard as that may be to believe from your standpoint… And, yes, when I say *our* people, I am including you."

"Well, when I say my people, I am talking about my fri…" The word was right there on the tip of her tongue, and still she had trouble saying it. "Friends." She hadn't really had friends in so long. But that was what they were.

"And I mean to include them too. But for the Council's sake, filter… okay?"

Mira sighed. He was right. "I'll be as nice as I can be."

The quiet serenity of Caldera Grove made an impression on more than just Mira. She caught the same sparkle in Lucian's moss-green eyes that she'd had on her first visit. This city was unlike anything she'd seen before. Even in her early human days on the farm, she'd never experienced such oneness with nature, and no doubt Lucian, Curtis, and Sarah never had either. Raised in New Haven's concrete jungle, the lush green nature-loving city contrasted so sharply it bordered on unbelievable. Patchwork carpets of lush green grass surrounded the buildings, creating a gentle buffer between each and the road they walked on. Trees sprang up unobstructed, some even growing through the houses near which they had taken root. Branches jutted out oddly from walls with special holes in them to give the tree room to grow over time. This closeness with nature had perplexed and intrigued Mira the first time she'd seen it. Now, seeing it through the eyes of her companions seared into her mind how utterly different these two races had become. That planted tiny seeds of doubt in her mind. *What if the humans and the Otherkin could not get along? What if their differences were insurmountable?* She was preparing to risk life and limb going back to the human city, but her human friends here could be in peril.

Doubt and worry had been foreign concepts to Mira in the past. And that was how she liked it. These new protective feelings caused a small uncomfortable pang in her chest.

She'd rather be fighting than constantly concerned for the wellbeing of others. Tedious and troublesome worries dampened her sharp edge, and she needed to be on her game when they headed back to New Haven.

"How long have you all been here?" Lucian's amazement could not be contained.

"Since just after the Iron Gates were built." Stryker's tone did not betray any emotion. Even if it had, Mira doubted Lucian was truly listening. He had wandered over to a large garden and was admiring the flowers still open and reaching up to the moonlight.

Childlike in innocence, he almost squealed in delight as he bent down to touch the soft petals. Moonlight might have muted the pinks, yellows, and purples, but that did not seem to dampen his appreciation of them. Lucian plucked a large five-petal white and yellow flower.

Before he could stand and turn with his new treasure, Stryker was on him. "What the hell do you think you're doing?"

Lucian wasn't the only one confused by the wolf's sudden aggression. "Sorry. I just…" His eyes frantically searched for a safe place to land and when they met Mira's, Lucian scrambled over to her. "A flower for the lady."

All the highborn Elite rose right to the surface, washing away the awkwardness he'd shone only moments prior. He held the flower to Mira. "Please… for you."

Now she was truly confused. Did she look like the kind of girl you gave a flower to? What was he playing at?

Silent moments passed with him holding the flower and Mira standing frozen in her spot looking utterly confused, not wanting to take it.

Stryker took a deep loud breath. "We do not remove the flowers from their place, so that all may enjoy their beauty."

"My apologies." Lucian addressed Stryker, but his gaze was fixed on Mira.

"I don't want the flower," Mira finally said, relieved to have a legitimate reason to reject the offered gift. "Especially if it will piss off our hosts."

Lucian put the small flower through the button hole of his shirt. "We come from different cultures. Giving a flower is…"

Stryker cut him off. "I don't care about your ways. We are not in your city. What grows in the ground has its own purpose. Flowers are beautiful to look at and provide pollen for the bees – who in turn provide us with honey as well as continual pollination. It is a cycle that should not be broken just for the sake of turning a pretty woman's eye."

Testosterone and the unchecked aggression between the two men were beginning to get on Mira's nerves.

"Perhaps we can just move on." Sarah's small voice seemed to do the trick. Both men snapped to attention. Mira was never more thankful for the interruption she provided.

Stryker's temper subsided. He turned to the older human woman, his voice much calmer. "Yeah. Keep heading down this road. We're nearly there."

Lucian moved quickly to rejoin his two human friends, and Stryker matched pace with Mira.

"Didn't you just tell me to be nice, not five minutes ago?" Mira asked.

"Yes… to the Council. Your friends are not that important."

"Careful, wolf. They are important to me."

Unfazed by her warning tone, Stryker shrugged. "No matter. They will have to learn out ways. Play by our rules, if they plan to co-exist here."

She couldn't argue that fact. This place went beyond culture shock… in a good way, and would take a lot of getting used to. "They will. Give them time. What is your problem with Lucian, anyway?"

"He's human."

She turned a knowing eye on him. "It goes beyond his humanity. You only prickle like this when he's around me."

"He has feelings for you."

"So?" She'd thought the same thing, but that didn't matter much to her. She'd never dared to open her heart again. Not since Theo's death all those years ago. Emotions were messy and more painful than any lightbox the humans could concoct.

"He's human."

"You've said that."

"He has no business having feelings for an Otherkin."

"Really?" Not that she was putting herself on the market, but she didn't much like the wolf's implication that Lucian's species took him out of the running. The fact that Stryker claimed her to be of his kind, though, really threw her off guard. She'd never really felt she *belonged* anywhere before. "Is that all?"

Stryker hesitated. "Yes."

Mira had to hold back her snickering. She rather enjoyed seeing the wolfman trying hide whatever it was he was feeling.

"Well. Feelings are pretty useless things anyways. And besides that, I'm not spoken for, so whoever wants to have feelings can have them. I'm certainly not going to stop them."

If an Alpha could look wounded, Stryker was making a good attempt. Either way, it wasn't a good look for him. Maybe she'd struck a nerve with him. He couldn't really harbor feelings for her. He'd only just met her. She scoffed silently. *Feelings are such messy things.*

The hurt extended to Stryker's tone. "If feelings are so useless, then why didn't you take the flower he offered you?"

Mira shrugged, more to herself than in response to his question. Why hadn't she taken it? Lucian looked terribly awkward holding it. She knew he'd been offering it as a kindness, but somehow, doing it in front of Stryker felt so wrong. "What am I going to do with a flower? Hold it while it dies?"

Stryker smiled and tousled her black hair playfully. "You could place it in your hair."

She couldn't contain her laughter. "You're kidding, right? What kind of girl do you think I am? Next you're going to tell me I should wear a dress." *That'll be the day.*

"I can see why you're not accustomed to people having feelings for or around you. You lack any girlish qualities."

"Is that supposed to insult me?"

"Did it?"

"You'll have to try harder than that."

"Only if you give me plenty more opportunities to do that."

Now who was the one playing games with feelings? That odd awkward sensation came back, doubly so when she spotted Lucian's concerned expression. He'd stopped short and stood with his arms crossed, watching like a man ready to go to war.

"Something wrong?" Mira asked, but she had the sneaking suspicion she knew the answer.

"Just concerned... wondering how we should go about things... with regard to the meeting." All diplomat, but Lucian's tone spoke volumes of what he really wanted to say. He was just as annoyed with her talking to Stryker as the wolf had been with Lucian's interactions with her.

"You'll do best to let me and Mira handle things." Diplomacy had left Stryker, and his response dripped with condescension. "Speak when spoken to. Be brief and respectful."

Lucian's lips pursed tight. His nostrils flared with each breath, but he held his tongue.

The testosterone was thick enough to choke her, and she needed to snap these two idiots out of it. "Lucian's input is invaluable," Mira said. "He is, after all, an Elite of the city. That brings with it some important inside information. He will speak when he has need to. And so will our friends." She motioned toward Curtis and Sarah.

Hints of apprehension flashed in their eyes. Sarah sighed. "We don't want to cause any trouble." She clung tightly to her husband. "We're just glad for the chance to have a home and will do whatever is needed of us."

"And that is exactly what the Council needs to see. Humans are not the enemy. They can co-exist." Mira was never more proud to have Sarah along. They might have gotten off to a rocky start, but she'd proven many times over that she was an asset. "Now, we just need to make sure you and Lucian set that example too." She glared at Stryker.

He met her eyes, staring back with all the power of his Alpha status behind him. "I will do my part. You make sure to be polite – all of you – and we will get through this."

"Oh… I'll kill them with kindness."

That snapped the Alpha from his dominance stare and in an instant, the aggression faded into genuine amusement. "I'd like to see you try."

CHAPTER THREE

As before, the moment she walked inside of the large dome-shaped Capitol building, the ominous pressure of her task began to weigh heavily on her. Something about it, maybe the official nature of the place, the order of it, gave her pause.

The long, slender receptionist, Selene, stood immediately upon their arrival. Ignoring the trio of humans and Mira, she batted her long eyelashes at Stryker. "You're late. The council has been waiting. But I'll bet they can forgive you this once."

The sickeningly sweet way she spoke to him made Mira want to gag. Thankfully, Stryker was all business, cutting off what would have most likely have been more simpering conversation by walking straight to the elevators. "We'll head up, then."

Mira and the others followed without giving a second glance to Selene. Mira was sure the Otherkin woman felt the slight, but she didn't bother to look back and satisfy herself by seeing the angered expression.

By the time they reached the Council chambers, all signs of animosity between Lucian and Stryker had faded. Uniting against a common foe will do that; something Mira had learned in the arena many years ago. Everything came down to putting on a good show – another skill Mira had learned in the arena. *Funny*, she mused. *Just another day… but in a different arena.*

Alec wasn't really her enemy, but neither was he friendly to her or the humans she called friends. Though obviously competing for her approval, Mira appreciated the way both Stryker and Lucian handled themselves, especially after seeing the hateful glare in Alec's eyes as they came to the door of the conference room.

The dwarf's displeasure was unmistakable, and he aimed it all directly at Mira. Not even giving the humans a second glance, his eyes bore into Mira's with the threat of death behind them. Sure, she'd thwarted his plan to have no human set foot in Caldera, breaking rules...that was something Mira excelled at, but her intentions were honorable. And the deal she'd made went well beyond the crime they accused her of committing. She did not deserve his ire, but had to hold back her own inner rage. *Put on a good show, that's all I need to do now. Nail down details to their plan and get the hell out of here. Should be simple.*

Without a word, Alec motioned for them to enter. The room was huge and filled by a table cut from a solid plank of natural wood, preserved in a high-gloss finish. "I'll gather the rest of the Council. Please. Make yourselves comfortable." His words were congenial enough, but the daggers his eyes shot at Mira spoke to his true feelings.

"I don't trust that guy," Lucian said, taking a presumptuous seat at the head of the table. "He agreed too quickly to let us in. He has an agenda."

"Of that I have no doubt," Mira agreed. "But we need shelter, and you need protection."

Maybe it was the way she said the word protection – she hadn't intended to insult him – but Lucian suddenly straightened in his seat, and the high-born Elite in him returned. "I appreciate your concern, but I can take care of myself."

Mira had to fight not to roll her eyes. *Men. Always having to prove they're the biggest and baddest. Stupid.* "Now's not the time for playing the tough guy. We all know you'd be dead in a week living out there in the badlands."

Lucian's expression cycled from embarrassed to appalled. He turned away from her, only to find Stryker's steely glare. When he opened his mouth to speak again, Mira cut him off before the sound escaped his lips. "Any human would be dead out there. The deal I made was to ensure you remained alive."

"And no one appreciates that more than we do," Lucian said, indicating Curtis and Sarah.

The older human male cleared his throat and stood proudly next to his wife. "Yes. We all appreciate what you have done. Never before could I have imagined that a vampire would be our savior. You've certainly show me the error of my thinking."

Sarah smiled. "Yes. Me as well. When we first met, I was hoping you'd burn in the daylight." Mira snickered. She'd certainly gotten that impression on their first encounter. "But you've saved me and my husband so many times in this last week. We owe you our lives."

The appreciation party was nice, but Mira didn't need to hear their thanks.

"Get on with the but."

Despite his aggravated expression, Lucian laughed. "Always so blunt. What we're getting at is… You've done a lot and we trust you, but be wary of the deals you make with the Otherkin."

Now it was Stryker's turn to look annoyed. "Why, is there something wrong with making a deal with my people?"

"Historically…" Lucian's hard glare softened. "At least what I was taught…"

"Oh, are you suddenly an expert on Otherkin? A week ago you hardly knew a thing about vampires, now you know about others?" Mira asked.

The high-born elite faded again. Lucian stuttered, tripping over his words. "No, not an expert. Just... there was mention of Otherkin in our history books. They were called tricksters."

Unimpressed, Mira narrowed her gaze on Lucian. "And I recall ... other information you knew to be true about my kind was nothing more than slander and prejudice."

"I'll not deny that I have my prejudices against the supernatural people."

Ready with an angry retort, Mira opened her mouth to speak, but Lucian held up a hand. "Those prejudices against your kind are unfounded. Those I have recently lost, but others have yet to be broken by deeds."

Mira scrunched up her face, confused, and suddenly filled with questions, but again, Lucian held his hand up as if to say, hush.

"As Regent of New Haven, I had the duty of sending patrols out. Some never came back. Some came back stark raving mad. I can only imagine it was Otherkin..." Lucian tried to suppress the sneer, but Mira saw it. "Like that muse who addled their brain."

"I'll take credit where credit is due." Alec's arrogant tone surprised the whole room. They'd all been too wrapped up in their own conversation to see he had returned with the rest of the Council, none of whom looked happy to be there. Alec sauntered over to a high chair that appeared to have been specially made for his petite stature. "We do what we must to protect our own. As a former leader yourself, I'm sure you can appreciate that." Shockingly, Alec not only addressed Lucian directly, but he was looking at him too.

"Many of those men, my human soldiers, never recovered." Lucian didn't bother hiding his anger.

"And many of our own patrols never came back," Alec shot back at Lucian. "They had families too you know."

The two looked as if they might come to blows. The idea of letting them, in the arena, flitted into Mira's mind. They didn't deserve a fight to the death, but men were always better knocking each other around for a bit before they could cool down and talk reason. At least, the men she'd known... half-starved vampires. These two, though claiming to be civilized, seemed no different.

At the rate they were all going, nothing was going to be accomplished. "Enough!" She hadn't intended to shout, but her voice seemed to have its own volume control "We've all wronged and been wronged here. The point is we need to find an end. Peace or whatever else we come up with."

"Peace may never come, but an end to the outright hostility and slavery of our people will suffice." Michael said. As the vampire representative on the council, he stood out with his pale skin and striking eyes. He glided across room almost as if he were not walking but merely floating above the ground, and took a seat in the middle edge of the table. "Please, let us sit and discuss things like civilized beings."

Though the word made her snicker a little, Mira was thankful at least someone on the Council was making the attempt at civility.

Natasha, the other vampire council representative, followed Michael's path just as regally and took her place next to her counterpart.

Mira waited to see if Natasha would add anything to the conversation, but the tall, dark-haired vampire was mute and looked as if she had better things to do than deal with Mira and her humans.

Roseanna joined her counterpart Alec at the table, sitting quietly, her expression neither passive nor aggressive. She'd always been fairly quiet, Mira recalled. Even in their previous dealings, the female Otherkin had been keener to watch and wait than jump in with emotional responses. Mira made a mental note to remember this about her. Appeal to her sense of factual data, perhaps, if the situation arose.

Niko the sharp-nosed and the redhead Katerina, both shifter elders, joined Lucian at the head of the table.

Mira wondered how deliberate their placement had been, forcing the others to filter in between them all. Another startling addition on which Mira picked up immediately were larger men, wearing green robes, guards perhaps, filtering into the room after the elders. The weapons at their side would suggest guardians or soldiers, but as before, Mira noticed that the blades they wielded were all as shiny as the day they were forged. Unused. Untested. They might be there as guards, or maybe as intimidation, but it wasn't working on Mira. Even if they packed the room with additional support, she'd wager she could still take them on and have a fighting chance. Untested soldiers were child's play for the well trained and battle worn.

"Please... sit," Michael said again.

Mira took Sarah and Curtis by the arms and pulled them with her to the table, taking places between the shifters and the vampires. Stryker took the closest available space near Mira, and members of his pack began to filter into the room after. Their presence shocked Mira. Back at the pack's den, no one had been around. She'd assumed they were on patrol or out hunting. After the shock subsided, something she had not felt in a long while settled down on her: warmth, like the comfort of a warm blanket. Security. Dare she admit it, a sense of solidarity.

Such an odd feeling; a good one, but very odd. Having people on her side. It bolstered her confidence more than she could possibly say. She met their eyes one by one and silently mouthed her thanks to them for showing up. And, one by one, they nodded in response.

With as many bodies as the room could hold, the whole mood became claustrophobic. Mira was used to crowds watching her from above, but elbow room only with potentially hostile people was disconcerting.

Not one for mincing words, Mira spoke up. "Is it necessary to pack the room so tightly?"

"At the moment, yes," Alec informed Mira archly. "We are here to discuss the details of our deal. Should anything go... poorly... we want assurances that we are safe."

"From a couple of humans?" Mira snorted.

"From you," Alec said flatly.

She hadn't expected that.

"I see you sizing up our guards. You've already swayed the allegiance of our patrolling pack."

Mira stood slamming her hands down on the table. "You seem quite happy to condemn me as the enemy. What grievous injury have I dealt you? All I've done is come here requesting sanctuary. As a vampire, that is my right, is it not?" She didn't wait for him to answer. "Yes, I brought humans with me. Yes, I know your rules say humans cannot come inside. But things are no longer black and white."

"Funny to hear that from a former slave." Alec snickered.

"All the better it come from a slave. I've witnessed firsthand the atrocities of the human race. I've been tortured, beaten, abused, and forced to kill my own kind... at the request of the humans. But, unlike you, I know that not everyone should be judged by their people's mistakes. These humans" – she placed a hand on Curtis and Sarah both, emphasizing her point — "they are good. They have proven that to me and to your patrolling wolf-pack. That is what swayed them, not me. You, however, have it stuck in your head that I am the enemy, rather than opening up your eyes to the fact that times have changed."

"I have seen no such goodness. What I have seen is half of our patrolling pack decimated, all after you and your humans appeared. This one" — Alec jabbed a finger at Lucia — "he's an Elite of their city. They are hunting him and you. Because of that, your presence threatens our way of life."

Mira grumbled. Mechanical and unfeeling, that's how Alec sounded. He'd not even bothered to truly look at the facts. All he cared about was getting rid of the humans... and Mira.

"And that is why I made your deal, Alec... to ensure my human friends' safety. I will take on the challenge of ending the Iron Gate's pursuit of us and your home, but you must ensure the safety of my friends. My *human* friends."

Alec opened his mouth as if to speak, but Mira beat him to the punch. "If you want our deal to stand, then end this open hostility." She waved a hand at the guards surrounding the table. "Get rid of them, and let's have a peaceful conversation."

Alec took a breath. His lips pursed tightly with pent-up rage. No words escaped, yet at a nod of his head, the guards turned and left the room.

"Now that the unpleasantness is over... Let's start fresh." Michael spoke up, since Alec remained silently seething. "We need troops if we're going to protect ourselves against the humans and any possible retaliation from our actions against them. Mira, you mentioned the other vampires imprisoned?"

She nodded, thinking of George and her promise to him to set him free. "Yes, there are many of my kind held below ground in the Iron Gate prison. I cannot guarantee all will want to fight for your cause, but plenty will want their revenge."

"Yes. Precisely. Their revenge aligns well with our needs. We could be valuable assets to one another. And of course we would extend the offer of sanctuary to all." Words carefully chosen by a seasoned politician. Michael didn't care what their motivation was as long as it met his ends, and Mira understood that clearly, especially when his contemplative eyes fixed on her. "It would be best if you could free them all."

"Easier said than done. The prison area is heavily guarded, but with Lucian's help" – she made it a point to emphasize his name – "I think we can manage. No one knows that place better than he."

Michael's brow crinkled. "But, he'll be a liability, will he not, being human and all?"

"As a human, he is weak. Yes." Mira glanced at Lucian speaking silently with her eyes, telling him not to disagree with her no matter what negative thing she said. She hoped he got the message. "Without his expertise, though, we will be lost. The prisons are built like a maze to keep those of us who have not learned their twists and turns inside. I've made many escape attempts in the past, and been thwarted by my own lack of direction."

"She's right." Lucian confidently spoke up. Clearly he had missed her message of silence. "You need me. As long as my access codes have not been canceled, I can not only guide you, but also help bypass security."

At least he was showing them his importance, though Mira had hoped he would let her do the talking.

Michael waved a dismissive hand. "Then it is settled. The human Lucian will return with you. What of these two here?" He pointed to Sarah and Curtis.

She kept her hands firmly planted on their shoulders, silently emphasizing to the room they were under her protection. "They stay behind, where they are safe." Mira's tone was cool with an undertone of warning. Curtis and Sarah had been through enough. They deserved some rest and recuperation, and more than that, to be safe.

"Fine, fine, they stay," Niko spoke up before Michael could.

Mira let go a loud sigh of relief. That, she had assumed, would be the hardest thing to secure. "And I have your word on this?"

"Fine." Neither his tone nor his expression betrayed his inner thoughts. If anything, he appeared bored by the matter.

"I need more than that."

"What, then?" Michael was at the edge of patience, and Mira spotted it quite clearly.

"I want your oath," she demanded. Though there was no guarantee of their safety once she was gone, she hoped their blood oath was truly as strong as had been implied.

"Fine, I said! I give my oath, they will remain safe," Michael huffed.

"No. Not just your oath. I want everyone's oath. These humans, the three of them, when under your protection of sanctuary, will have no harm come to them. Say it!"

Collective shock ran through the room. Even Stryker looked horrorstruck at her demand, but Mira was not about to back down.

Silent moments passed with uneasy tension. Mira did not let that waiver her resolve. She met the eyes of each council member individually and challenged them to back down from their deal.

"You have my blood oath," Alec begrudgingly agreed.

The rest followed one by one.

"Are we done with this business?" Michael's annoyance was plain. "The humans have taken up enough of our concern. As of now, you have two on your team... How many more will you need to return to the city and accomplish your task?"

Satisfied, Mira relaxed her grip on the two humans and let out a sigh of relief. "The smaller our group the better. Maybe two or three others to help take down the handlers... preferably not vampires. The handlers rely on UV weapons."

Both Michael and Natasha hissed at the sound of UV as a weapon.

"Yes, quite unpleasant. So, shifters would have the advantage here," Mira said.

"I and my pack are at your disposal." Stryker had already made the offer to her, but here it was made public, and that gave his statement added weight. Niko's lip curled slightly at his offer, but he did not say anything against it.

"Thank you, Stryker." Mira smiled at the amber-eyed wolf. His support meant more than she could really say. It was an honor and a privilege for her to go into this unknown with him. "That's all I need."

"As for the other two humans..." Alec finally broke his silence. "What use will they be to us while they are our wards?"

His tone bothered Mira, but she had his blood oath and would make damn sure he paid it if any harm came to them. "Curtis is a skilled electrician. He can help around here in the city while we're gone."

Curtis stood up. "I'm pretty handy with more than just electrical things. I'm what you might call a bit of a tinkerer. I can do a little of everything. Just tell me what of yours needs fixin', and I can take care of it."

"And the girl?" Alec narrowed his eyes on Sarah. Mira had to repress a sneer. Where the others were indifferent to her human friends, Alec, it seemed, had a singularly hateful interest in them.

Sarah cleared her throat and spoke up. "I have some first aid training. I can help with the wounded. And I can cook."

"Oh, yeah." The mention of cooking had Curtis practically salivating. "She can whip up meals to make your mouth water!"

"Fine." Alec sighed, unimpressed. "We will put their skills to use somehow, so they do not burden us."

A snide comment rested on the tip of Mira's tongue. Alec might have been a Council member and older than dirt, but his petty hatred was testing her last nerve. It wouldn't take much for her to snap his little neck. She had to push down the homicidal thoughts. Arrogant, annoying, and pompous as he was, he was technically on her side. "Burden or not… they are to be protected."

"I keep to my deals. You have already been given my blood oath. Let that be enough." Alec's tone bordered on angry, but that did not worry Mira.

"I'll hold you to that. And I'll have your blood… all of it… should any harm come to them." She wasn't taking any chances where the humans were concerned.

"Threats are not necessary." Michael's voice too carried undertones of anger, but he kept his face neutral. "The deal has been struck."

"Fine." It was anything but. However, her point had been made, and they did have more to arrange before she could be off. "Moving on. What equipment and weapons can you offer us?" They'd need more than their bare hands to fight into the human city. "We need to travel light and quick. It's at least two days by vehicle back to the city."

Michael's brow furrowed. "What vehicles we have are ones collected and rebuilt from the human patrols that have come through these parts over the last century. You'll have to leave the city to get to where they are stored. None have ever made it to our gates."

"But you do have some form of transport?" Mira asked, suddenly worried about how they were going to attempt this city siege.

Shrugging his shoulders, Michael responded, "We don't need them here in Caldera."

That wasn't an answer. She hoped for their sake a salvageable vehicle could be located. "Curtis, I might need you to come look at the vehicles before we go."

His chest puffed with sudden importance. "Not a problem, Mira. I'll make something work for you."

Natasha met Mira's concerned eyes and finally spoke. "Stryker can take you to the weapons hall. Use whatever you need. I'm sure something in there will make you happy. A new blade, perhaps?"

The idea of fresh steel in her hands brought a smile to Mira's worried face. A good weapon in hand did wonders for confidence. "Yes, please. A new sword would be lovely."

"You truly have a warriors spirit." Natasha smiled; though warm, it wasn't a genuine smile. There was something else behind her eyes. Mira couldn't quite place it, but she felt as if she were just a tool to meet their needs. That was probably the truth. She'd never really assumed she'd be welcomed in as kin. Her skills singled her out as a pawn in a bigger man's game, but rather than let that thought get her down, she shrugged it off. She had her own desires to realize too. Imagining the look on George's face when she opened his cell was enough to make her ready to go back to that hell hole.

"Okay, transportation is iffy. What about communication?" Mira asked.

"We still do that the old fashion way." Alec whistled.

Mira crinkled her brow in confusion.

The door opened and a small brown bird flew in from another room. It landed softly in the middle of the table in front of Alec. As soon as its little feet hit the polished wood, the bird transformed into a naked female, small enough to fit in the palm of Mira's hand, with bright red hair. The little woman smiled and hopped up into Alec's palm. He raised her to his ear and listened as she whispered a message. After she was finished, he nodded and returned her to the table.

"This is Jay," Alec said. "She and a few of her flock will act as messengers between us. When you have secured your troops, just whistle for her. She'll be following close behind you, and the humans will never suspect. Send word of your next move, and we will then join you and take on the humans from both sides!"

Jay winked at Mira and transformed back into her bird form. She flew up and perched on Mira's shoulder and whispered in her ear, "At your service!"

"Okay. I think we have all we need. Let's get going, then." Mira stood and motioned for her group to follow. "Soon as I have a look at the vehicle situation, we're out of here."

CHAPTER FOUR

Her beautiful stars twinkled above as she, Stryker, and Curtis hiked down the rocky path away from Caldera to the cave where old salvage transports were kept. She wondered if she'd ever tire of the serenity their light brought. No one else seemed to care. Taking them for granted. She supposed she had too once, before Theo had turned her. How many human years had she lived without truly appreciating them? And how many more had she been shut away from their silvery light? No, she'd not take them for granted ever again. And neither, she assumed, would her vampire brethren back in New Haven. Once she made it there to release them, they too would appreciate the beauty of freedom and the welcoming glow of a clear night sky.

That, of course, hinged on her actually getting back to New Haven quickly. Based on what she'd been told, getting her hopes up was only going to lead to disappointment. Still, they had to see if any of the old transports could be made to work long enough to get them back to New Haven. Given the distance between them and the Iron Gate, it could be as long as a week before she and her group could begin their mission if forced to do it on foot. And for her, almost double that, since she'd be forced to wait out the daylight in some kind of cave.

"Just over here." Stryker bounded over a large boulder and disappeared from view. "I've parked many a transport vehicle over the years. We don't like leaving things out in the forest. Makes the humans think they're getting close."

Curtis stumbled over the rocks, tripping a few times, but he made no complaints. Much to his credit, for a human he was very agile.

Mira followed Stryker's voice as she scrambled over the large rocks in the trail. "Smart." Her hopes were renewed noticing that he had said "parked" rather than "pushed."

"Most of our transports are solar powered," Curtis added. "Going to need a bit of light to get them going."

That complicated things a little. "So if they've been parked and its night time, how will we know they're going to run?"

If Curtis was worried, his voice didn't betray it. "I'll check under the hood. Make sure the wiring is all as it should be. Mechanics are pretty simple beasts, really."

Stryker stopped short and turned back towards Mira. Even in the dark she could see the amber of his eyes. "You'll just have to give it a little hope."

Was he mocking her? "Hope?" That wasn't a word she liked to use.

"Don't start with the negativity." Stryker chuckled at her angry pout. "You've done so many impossible things in this last week: fighting off the humans, escaping their city, getting your three human friends into Caldera. Luck, or something like it, is on your side. Be positive for a change."

Mira crossed her arms, wondering how many more times she'd have to hear that same speech. She was a realist in a world filled with dreamers, it seemed. "Positivity doesn't get you anything. Action does."

"Ray of sunshine, this one." Stryker elbowed Curtis as if they were old friends.

Despite the animosity Mira had encountered from the others, Stryker held no prejudices between them. Quite an endearing quality. Not unlike her friend Lucian, who had given up on many of his own prejudices after encountering Mira. If two enemies could become unlikely friends, maybe there was hope for some form of peace somewhere down the road.

Curtis chuckled. "Yeah, but she gets results."

His comment amused her, but Mira didn't want to let them know that. "*She* is right here. You don't need to speak of me as if I'm not."

Ignoring her haughty tone, Stryker continued, leading them down towards a small cave entrance. Nothing blocked the entry, no stones nor manmade doors, but the mouth of the cave was nearly invisible under the shadows created by moonlight. Stryker, however, knew exactly where to go. He walked them straight to the mouth of the cave without so much as a stumbling misstep.

No light found its way into the depths of the cave, but that did not stop Mira's vampire eyes from seeing outlines of what lay inside.

Stryker gathered items to make a torch while Mira ventured in for a closer look. Inside the cave was a musty cloying smell of old grease and mold. It turned her nose, and at the same time brought back memories of the prison level where she'd spent so much time. Not for the greasy smell, but mold and dust were two constants in the prison. Poor ventilation and dirty, sweaty mattresses were staples. Add a hint of blood in the air and she might have sworn she was back in her cell. Suddenly, she felt the walls closing in and wanted out of the cave.

Turning to leave, she saw Stryker with the torch. As quickly as the feeling had come, seeing her new friend and the orangey glowing light washed it away.

"You okay, Mira?" He asked.

"Fine," she lied. "Just not sure what to look for."

Stryker walked around the cave, lighting wall-mounted torches to illuminate the walls.

While the mouth of the cave had been smallish – no bigger than the size of a transport vehicle – inside seemed cavernous. Although spacious, it was crammed with all manner of vehicles. Small two-wheeled ones, large ones on tracks, small speeders with seating space for four, and even one that looked as if it might fly.

"Wow!" Curtis exclaimed. Eyes wide like a child who'd just walked into a toyshop, he practically stuttered with excitement. "A VT2?" He ambled over to a particularly large propeller vehicle and patted its metallic body like an old family pet.

"A what?" Mira asked, wondering what language he'd just spoken.

"Vertical Transport!" Curtis's eyes lit up as he ran his hand along the length of the vehicle's body. "I haven't seen one of these babies in years."

That piqued her interest. "Vertical, as in flying?"

"Shot it down a few years ago. Doesn't work, I'm afraid," Stryker added. He stood in the center of the room, arms crossed, letting Curtis and Mira have room to explore.

"You shot it down? With what weapons?" She shot a quizzical look to her shifter friend. Not that she'd had much experience with the Otherkin, but she hadn't noticed any weapons other than the ones the humans brought. Swords and daggers seemed to be the choice weapons for the citizens of Caldera.

Stryker returned her questioning gaze with an impish grin. "This one got as far as this cave. Pulled out that old tank and emptied a few shells into the big beast's belly. Leaked something awful and then" – he mimed shooting at the big vehicle then smashed his fist into his palm – "it practically fell from the sky."

Curtis nodded thoughtfully, eyes still locked onto the big metal beast of a transport. "That don't surprise me. The VT2s had engine issues. The propellers took too much energy to run, and solar cells couldn't provide the right oomph. These guys here," he continued, patting the vehicle lovingly, "they're a hybrid model. Second edition. Added fuel engines to help get the needed push." Curtis ducked down and fingered a few holes along the bottom of the body. "Course, if you hit that fuel line and drained it... no more propeller. Bet this one made a nice loud little boom when it crashed."

She could only imagine seeing that hulking metal beast flying through the air. The mental image of it falling out the sky was hard to fathom. "But you said you hadn't seen them in years. They aren't used anymore?"

Curtis shook his head. "Problem with them is they're too costly to run, and they have horrible maintenance issues. A few newer models are still in limited use. Magistrate uses them to travel between the eight cities, but other than that, no... not common. And this baby here... will never kiss the sky again."

"Well, there goes the idea of flying in." Her shoulders slumped. Flying would have been a novel treat. But it was probably better they stick to the ground anyway. "Let's locate something armored... and large enough to take the whole group in." Mira wandered through the available vehicles, keeping an eye out for anything that resembled the one in which she'd arrived. Roof mounted guns would be a plus, along with sun blocking armor. She could safely sleep the day away while others took shifts.

Most were broken or badly damaged. Some looked as if they'd been through a war, but after a half hour of weeding through, Mira found one. Smaller than she'd hoped for, but still with room for five people. And the only windows were in the front. She could make do with covering up in the back of the vehicle if need be. "Curtis. Here. Check this one out."

He rushed over excitedly. "Oh, yes, this will do nicely. Light and fast. They don't make them like this anymore either." He looked like he'd hit the jackpot, eyeballing the vehicle in front of them. "See how aerodynamic the design is? No bulky weaponry sticking out. Yes. This will get you there quick."

"What if we encounter trouble on the road?" Stryker asked.

"You'll have to outrun them." Curtis could hardly take his eyes off the vehicle. He ran a hand along the line of the roof and then down toward the door handle. "This one was built for speed."

With the push of the handle the door opened, swinging up-wards rather than out to the side. Mira jumped back.

"I'll check it out and disable any tracking devices that may still be inside."

Happy they'd found something, Mira let herself get cautious-ly hopeful. "How long before you'll know if it works?"

"It'll have to charge up a bit before I can know anything for sure, but I'd say, if the solar cells are still good, you'll be ready to leave tomorrow night. We'll let her charge up during the day while you sleep."

"Let's get her outside then." Stryker walked around the vehi-cle. "You steer, I'll push." He shot a wink in Mira's direction and she wasn't too sure why.

"I'll help you push too." Mira followed Stryker around the back of the transport.

Their combined strength made quick work of moving it beyond the mouth of the cave. Out in the open, it could bathe in the sun all day long and with any luck fill its solar cells for the journey.

Hopeful that they'd have transportation, Mira took a step back and dusted her hands. "I'll head back and pack our things. We'll meet here tomorrow night and be off."

Stryker nodded. "I'll stay here with Curtis and get things running. Do you remember the way back?"

"I think I can manage." She had plenty of fresh footprints to follow and Curtis's lingering smell to help guide her back up the mountain. Feeling a little more confident about their journey now, Mira was almost eager to get on the way.

CHAPTER FIVE

O**ne working transport,** a small cadre of warriors, and enough knives and swords to equip them all. Mira and her team were as prepared as they could be to head back into the Iron Gate territory. Wasting no time, they sped through the badlands as soon as the sun had set, each taking turns driving through the day and night toward New Haven City.

Though prepared as she could be, Mira felt hindered by her own weaknesses. Forced to take shelter every morning, she was unable to drive as long as the other members of the group. Hiding behind a blanket just made her feel silly, too. More than once she caught a mocking stare from the wolves accompanying them.

Despite the speed of their transport, the trip back to New Haven felt as if it took days longer than it should have. Neither Stryker nor Lucian seemed to mind much. At least no one made any complaints, other than being trapped in close quarters, but Mira felt on edge the entire time.

During the time she was supposed to be sleeping, her mind wandered to George and the other vampires, trapped within the confines of the Iron Gate prison. Mira wondered if she'd truly be able to do what had been requested of her. The task seemed an insurmountable beast. Talking about it was one thing, but actually making their way back into the city was pure insanity, even for an accomplished warrior like her. She'd never been accused of being the most "with it" of individuals though, so crazy as it was, this plan was par for the course of her life. Still, though, as much a warrior as she was, a small thread of fear coiled deep within her, planting roots in her mind. Death was just beyond the horizon, and the taste of freedom and peace she'd been given might be all she'd get to enjoy in this life.

Before the fear grew wild, she forced the tone of her thoughts to more positive things. George. The look on his face when she released him would be worth all the lightboxes in the world. He'd told her countless times that she'd never escape. He'd have to eat his words when next they saw each other. And, she'd make good on her promise to free him, too. She smiled inwardly. Companions in enslavement, he'd been the closest thing to a brother to her.

"What's got you all smiley?" Lucian's voice broke her silent contemplation.

"Just thinking of freeing my people."

"Well, don't you sound like the optimistic freedom fighter now." His words might have been spoken in jest, but there was warmth behind them.

"If I don't try to stay positive, the truth of how impossible our task is will take over."

"Such a ray of sunshine…" Stryker appeared in front of her and sat roughly down on the transport's floor.

"Who's driving?" Lucian might have tried to hide it, but Mira caught the sneer in his voice.

"Turn around and look, why don't you? It's not driving itself." Stryker sounded more annoyed than tired. He didn't even bother looking up at Lucian to direct his irritated glare.

Great, more male testosterone and posturing. Really not what she needed at the moment. Everyone had to have to have their head in the game, and she'd make them understand that – the hard way – if they kept up their little pissing matches.

"How close are we to the city?" Mira snapped at both of them.

"Not long now. We just passed a dam. I'm going to assume that's their local water supply and possibly power source too. The city shouldn't be too far. We should see the wall shortly." The animosity left Stryker's voice when he addressed her.

She retained her aggravated tone. "Well, then, let's focus on important things, shall we? Do we have a plan for when we get there? No doubt the city gates will be well guarded and have constant surveillance."

"If we attempt to enter through the Elite's entrance, we should have less trouble. It's a little-known entrance to the city," Lucian said, more for Stryker's benefit than hers.

As the city walls appeared out of the front windows, a sense of urgency began to well within Mira. That wasn't going to work. Mira shook her head as she spoke. "But they know you're Elite. That changes things. Those entrances will be under more scrutiny in case you were stupid enough to return."

"Point taken. The only other entrance that should be quiet is used for maintenance and repair of the city walls. There's a small doorway. It's going to be out of the way, along the southernmost wall." Lucian pointed out of the vehicle's windshield, but the city was still too far away for her to accurately judge landmarks. She'd just have to take his word for it.

Stryker too. He nodded thoughtfully, scanning the horizon. "Stop here," he ordered the driver. The transport came to rest beside a thick tree trunk. Where once a vast forest must have been, only shells remained. Some trees still stood, but most had died or been cut down to be used in the nearby city. What remained were gnarly stumps, holes, rocks, and dirt.

"I'll take my wolves and we can scout the wall," Stryker offered.

"Be careful," Mira warned. "Go in wolf form and try not to be seen."

"We're not accustomed to seeing wolves in these parts. Your presence might alert someone," Lucian said.

"My team knows how to hunt in stealth. We'll be fine." Stryker looked down his nose at the Elite human, amber eyes narrowing with angered focus.

"Hey." Mira snapped her fingers in front of Stryker. "We're just looking out for you."

"Right…"

Mira caught the slight flush of red on Stryker's cheeks. *He should feel embarrassed,* she thought. All this stupid aggression between them was going to get someone killed. "Get your head in the game."

"Sorry. I'm just not used to taking orders from… others." He turned to Mira, softening his tone before he spoke again. "I didn't mean to come off as ungrateful for your suggestion for our protection. We'll be careful."

"It's okay. We're all on the same team." She reached out and lightly touched his shoulder. "We've got to look out for each other."

"Yes. We do." The ghost of a smile flashed across his face before disappearing. "I'll be fine. And when I get back, I'll have a full report on what we're up against." He turned away from her and Lucian.

The time for words had ended, obviously. With an almost imperceptible nod of his head, Stryker and the rest of his wolves stripped down and shifted into their wolf form. Though she meant to be *all business*, she couldn't help but watch with admiration as the well-toned men shifted and took off heading, south toward the city.

Above her, Mira heard the soft tweets of a bird. She looked out of the transport and saw the little brown Jay perched in a nearby tree. For a moment, she could have sworn she and the bird exchanged a look, and then off little Jay went, chasing after Stryker and the wolves.

Lucian followed the wolves' path outside of the transport but did not venture too far. He stood, surveying his surroundings, and stretched his arms high above his head. Taking a deep breath, he let out a long sigh. "If I didn't know any better, I'd say he doesn't like me much."

"Why would you say that?" Mira joined Lucian, taking a breath of fresh night air. "He helped keep you guys from being killed for trying to enter Sanctuary. And he didn't force me to turn you. If he hates you, that's a pretty funny way of showing it."

"Oh, I didn't mean it like that," Lucian said.

"Well, what did you mean?"

"Just that I might be in the way a bit here. That's all."

"Nonsense. We need you, and he knows it. You're just feeling a little useless right now because you're stuck here waiting with me," Mira said.

"I'm more than happy to be stuck, as you say, here with you. I do enjoy your company." Lucian sat down on a log and patted a spot next to him. "Join me and let's take a rest while the wolves do their thing."

"Thanks." She took the spot next to Lucian. Together they gazed out into the starry sky above the loose canopy of trees. "I feel like that's all I've been doing lately. Rest. Wait. Sit. I'm eager to see a little action."

"Miss life in the arena?" Lucian asked.

"Not the brutality, no. But the feeling of accomplishing something. Knowing I was the best. Proving it. That part. Being useful in some fashion. Freedom is great, don't misunderstand me, but I have yet to do anything with it."

"I'd say you've done quite a bit, and have much more to come." Lucian turned his soft green eyes on her. The depth of his state and the sincerity behind it gave her chills. The feelings he stirred within her were uncomfortable. What was he doing to her? A girl who could stare down a wolf for dominance couldn't maintain eye contact with a human? She was forced to turn away from his gaze.

Silence between them became awkward. Mira searched for something to say but came up empty. All of her thoughts were on the mission and trying to avoid getting killed.

Lucian finally spoke again. "If all goes well, you'll be the savior of your people. That's pretty important." His tone betrayed his underlying embarrassment, but his face was a mask of calm, eyes still locked onto Mira.

"That's a great big if. We still have to get inside. Then find some way to release the prisoners, rally them, and get them out of the city to rendezvous with the rest of the Otherkin."

"Well, when you put it like that…"

"It sounds impossible?"

"No, just involved. That's quite the to-do list." Lucian laughed uncomfortably.

"I'm glad you find the humor in the suffering of my people," Mira said.

"Hey, now. I'm on your side, remember."

Mira narrowed her eyes, scrutinizing Lucian's face. "Are you?"

"Seriously? You're going to question my loyalties now?" Lucian looked concerned.

Mira tried to hold her piercing gaze, but laughter bubbled up her chest. "Had you there for a minute, didn't I?"

Lucian let out a sigh. "A bit, yeah. That's one hell of a scary look you gave me."

"Well, if I can scare a Regent, maybe we have a chance."

CHAPTER SIX

A wolf howl pierced the silence Mira and Lucian had been enjoying. At first, she thought nothing of the sound, but after a moment she wondered at its meaning. They hadn't set up any type of code. Stryker, as she understood it, was just going to look around and come back. If he was howling, maybe he'd found trouble.

Mira jumped to her feet and ducked back into the transport for her sword and rucksack. "We better go see what's up."

"Wait, what if it's a trap? Shouldn't we wait for them to come back?" Lucian asked.

Dozens of terrible scenarios played out in her mind. She knew the atrocities the humans were capable of; she'd lived them. The wolves might only have seconds to live, if they weren't being killed off already. "I'm not waiting to find out."

Clearly not as worried as she, Lucian slowly stood. "You go on ahead. I'll catch up."

"Don't get caught," Mira warned, and then shouldered the rucksack and took off toward the direction from which the wolf had howled.

It didn't take her long to locate Stryker. He shifted from his wolf form as she approached.

"Where's Lucian?" Stryker asked.

Mira tossed him a pair of pants from her bag. "He's on his way. I thought you might have been hurt." Mira suddenly realized how stupid she'd been to leave the most vulnerable member of their group alone.

"No, I'm fine. I just needed to get your attention. This entrance to the main part of the city looks fairly easy. Only two guards on patrol, and I see only one security camera. We need to hurry, though; I spotted a roaming vehicle circling around earlier."

"Everything is too quiet. I wouldn't be surprised if we saw more on foot. The lower town isn't far away, and it's sure to be filled with soldiers. I doubt the main city would be so lax as to leave them to their own while the rest of the people are under such strict lock and key."

"Excellent point."

Soldiers. Patrolling all around. And she'd left Lucian to his fate. If anything happened to him, she'd never forgive herself. "I'd better go back and make sure Lucian gets here safe."

"He'll be fine," Stryker said.

He'd made it blatantly clear he didn't like Lucian because of the latter's interest in her, but the casual way he'd said that made her wonder if he secretly hoped Lucian might be cut out of the picture all together.

Mira glared down at him angrily. "You certainly sound sure of yourself."

Stryker sniggered at her. "Well, yes, I am. Because he's right behind you."

Mira hadn't been paying attention, but as soon as Stryker mentioned it, she heard his footsteps through the grass behind her. She didn't need to turn to see him. She felt ashamed for being so inattentive to her surroundings. "Guess I need to be more on my game tonight, huh?"

"If you want us all to survive, sure," Stryker said playfully.

Lucian came up quickly behind them. "Where are your other wolves?"

"They're flanking our position, ready for me to give the signal to move in," Stryker replied.

Lucian nodded. "This is a good spot. Through that gate we'll have access to the water treatment plant. If we can get inside, there are tunnels that should take us down through to the arena and the lower prison levels."

"Two guards here and a security camera are all that stand in our way," Mira said. "What do we do about the camera?" Surely that would alert someone to their presence and send the whole swarm of human guards down on them before they could get in deep enough.

Lucian shrugged casually. "This time of night surveillance is done via recording, unless the Magistrate has ordered otherwise. But I highly doubt they're expecting us to come back."

"We cannot take any chances. We need to assume the Magistrate has ordered manned surveillance round the clock," Mira said.

"Well…" Lucian blew out a breath. "Then there might be someone on camera, meaning there will be an instant alert if anything funny happens."

Mira mentally prepared for the fight, pushing down the knot of fear building in her chest. She knew this was a suicide mission. How long she and the others survived would be the question.

"How long will we have before reinforcements arrive?" Stryker said. If he was worried, his voice did not betray the feelings, nor was there any hidden fear in his eyes. He looked as calm and cool as Mira wished she could feel. Staring down death as if it were nothing. Maybe he was more the warrior than she.

Lucian, however, did not hide his concern. Hints of worry leeched into his words. "If they know where we're headed, they'll have a whole garrison on us in under ten minutes."

"But they might not know, so if we rush and gain access to the tunnels, they'll still be scrambling by the time we reach our prisoners." Mira tried to hold on to some small thread of hope. If all else failed, she was still going to free her friends.

"We have to assume that once an alert is raised, the prison will go on full lockdown," Lucian said grimly.

Mira nodded. "What's our plan, then?"

Lucian pinched the bridge of his nose and looked down to the ground. Mira wondered if he'd given up, but then, after a few silent moments, he took a deep breath and looked up again. Mira caught the spark of hope in his eyes. "Assuming my access codes still work," he said, "if you can keep me alive, I can get the cell doors open. Once they're open, it will be up to you, Mira, to make sure the vamps fight on our side."

Well, it wasn't perfect, but it was something. And something was better than the alternative. "Sure, as long as you disable the lights. If those come on, we're done."

Lucian nodded. "That will be the first thing I disable, then."

"Okay, Stryker. Send in your wolves." Mira reached down and gripped the hilt of her short sword. "Let's get this game going."

Though he was still in his human form, Stryker howled long and loud, piercing the stillness of the night. The guards waiting at the door were visibly alarmed by the sound. Lights clicked on in their hands; Mira recognized the UV torches and ducked behind Lucian incase the light somehow reached her.

She turned to look away and caught sight of one of the two flanking wolves sprinting into action. Like big moving blurs of color, they headed straight for the soldiers who were brandishing their lights like weapons.

Mira watched with an eager smile as the wolves they overtook the humans, dragging them to the ground kicking and yelling. She hoped their pitiful wails wouldn't alert any patrols on foot, but she wasn't about to wait and find out.

Enticed by the smell of fresh blood on the air, Mira was on her feet and moving. "Let's go," she said, and pulled Lucian with her.

They made a bee line for the entrance. Mira wasted no time and scooped up one of the fallen soldiers. Barely clinging to life, he was unconscious and limp in her arms, but his heart was still beating and blood trickled from his wounds. Perhaps she should have had a little decorum around Lucian, but days of hunger and an eagerness to taste fresh blood had her diving at the soldier's neck with wild abandon. Nothing was better than fresh blood, warm and straight from the vein, a delicacy she hardly ever got to enjoy. Mira savored its coppery tang, picking up small notes of sweetness as well.

As much as she enjoyed the rare treat, she knew she couldn't waste any more time. Sating her hunger, Mira dropped the soldier to the ground and wiped her mouth clean before turning to see Lucian and Stryker.

"What are you waiting for?" she snapped at the gawking pair. Really, what did they expect from her? She was a vampire, after all.

Stryker took a moment but found his voice faster than Lucian. "Just letting you enjoy your dinner."

"You'll be dessert if you don't stop staring at me. You two should have been breaking down this door." Mira snatched up the discarded gun from the dead soldier. She aimed and shot a camera above the door that had no doubt captured the gruesome scene. "Do I have to handle everything here? Get that door open." She gestured at Lucian, who still stood dumbstruck.

No alarm bells had sounded... yet. That wasn't exactly reassuring, though; silent alarms were what she feared. Not knowing when or where the danger was coming from added to her worry. Gun in hand and sword still at her side, she was ready for a fight.

"Access codes, blunt force, whatever. Just get it open and us inside... Now!" Mira kept her eyes on the horizon, but the order was clearly meant for Lucian.

No one was coming yet, but that didn't mean they wouldn't. Mira kept a fierce watch as Lucian went to work pushing buttons on the console next to the door.

"Not working. Blunt force might be our next best option." Lucian's tone bordered on frantic.

"Fine." Mira turned and threw her shoulder into the door. Once. Twice. Three times... nothing happened. Lucian kept plugging away at the control pad, entering various combinations of digits.

"Stryker, throw your weight into this too," she called to him.

Together they prepared to slam into the door, but just before they lunged forward, Lucian shouted, "Wait!"

The door slid open.

CHAPTER SEVEN

T hey'd hardly made it through the door before it slammed
shut behind them. But at least they had made it.
A bird twittered as it flew overhead – Jay, their little messenger,
probably heading back to the Otherkin with the news that they'd
made it inside. Stryker responded, whistling a few notes back, but
did not look up. He kept his vision locked on their immediate
surroundings.

"Where to now?" Mira asked, feeling a little uneasy. Inside
the great wall, she'd expected to enter the tunnels, but instead she
found herself in an open field. The edge of New Haven city lay
before her, but from where they stood, it had to have been at
least a mile away. The closest buildings looked like ancient ruins
from a time before the great cataclysm: half torn-down structures,
rusting in places where metal doors had once stood. A few
buildings looked intact but like a great wind might topple them.
To her left, mountains of trash stood as high as the wall itself,
and automated machines shuffled around debris into what
appeared to be great incinerators.

Too many moments of silence passed without an answer.
Mira turned to Lucian. "C'mon! Which way?"

The confused look on his face did not reassure her in the
slightest. "Hold on. Just getting my bearings."

Patience was not her strong suit, and anticipation only amplified her frantic feelings. "We don't have time for that. You were supposed to know where we were headed."

"Just because I was Regent does not mean I know every inch of this city. I was never a maintenance worker. I was Elite. I didn't venture into this dirty side of town, only viewed the maps of it. If you'll calm down and be patient, I'll figure it out, but it's going to take me a moment."

Lucian's condescending tone was the last thing they needed at that moment, and Mira was just about to put his pompous ass back in his place when Stryker spoke up. "We may not have a moment. That camera caught everything before Mira took it out. They know where we are and what we are – of that I have no doubt."

Mira pulled the rucksack from her back and tossed a soldier's uniform at Stryker. He donned it quickly. She had uniforms for the other wolves too, if they were ordered to shift to human. For now they waited patiently at the side of their leader. Stryker took the rucksack from Mira and threw it on his back.

After what felt like too long a time, Lucian's eyes lit with renewed energy. "There," Lucian said, pointing to one of the free standing buildings nearby. At the front was a pair of large rolling metal doors; an old loading bay, perhaps. "If I remember correctly, that should be our way into the underground maintenance tunnels."

"Let's hope you're right." Mira's impatient tone lessened somewhat, but still she felt the anxiety inside. Fighting didn't scare her, it was the unknown of what lay before her that had her twitching and jumpy.

"You two. Shift. Protect the human at all costs," Stryker ordered the wolves next to him. He dropped the rucksack on the ground, spilling out the clothes and a couple of daggers.

The other two wolves shifted, taking on their human appearances, and quickly put their uniforms on. "Stay in between us." Rob, the first wolf said to Lucian. Terrance, the other wolf, said nothing, but nodded to his partner as he sheathed a dagger at his belt, ready for action.

Lucian stuck close to his protection as they all headed towards what they hoped would be the entrance.

Rusted shut, this door had clearly not been used in quite some time. Mira questioned if it was in fact the maintenance back door that Lucian had said it was. Rather than add more fuel to the frustration between them, though, she remained quiet and put her efforts into getting inside the building. There was no way to open it silently, given its condition; she was quite sure the metal shriek it made as she forced it upwards would alert anyone within a mile of their location.

"So much for our stealthy entrance." Stryker said, but there was no laughter in his voice.

"Couldn't be helped," Mira said.

"It was a route used by the original settlers of this town. This old building was part of a shopping center before the great cataclysm. All these buildings were interconnected and had tunnel systems built into them to begin with. They helped to lay the framework for our city's infrastructure," Lucian said.

"I'd heard about people using them as fallout shelters during the great cataclysm," said Mira, impressed that buildings as old as these would still stand in some fashion.

"Some were able to take shelter in these, in areas less damaged during the quakes and storms, but most weren't so lucky," Lucian said.

"Is that the reason this city is here? It was one of the few places that was not hit that hard?" Mira asked. She'd been around for many years herself, but the great cataclysm had happened more than a hundred years before her birth. She often wondered what life had been like before it. Stories she'd grown up with had spoken of great cities and the entire continent filled with people. All she had known were the eight Iron Gate cities and their satellite farm communities. Everything else was badlands, supposedly uninhabitable.

"Yes. Our history books speak of…"

"Guys, I hate to break up the lesson, but let's move," Stryker said.

Embarrassed that curiosity had gotten the better of her, Mira's face flushed red. "Sorry, yes. Inside." She ushered them in and let the rusty door fall shut behind her. The place was pitch black, but that wasn't a problem for Mira. She could see outlines and shapes of objects. She might not have perfectly clear vision, but she'd not trip over anything in the dark.

"Can any of you guys see?" she asked.

"Wolves have excellent night vision," Stryker responded.

"Someone please guide me." Frustration filled Lucian's voice.

Mira heard someone trip and fall on the concrete ground, and assumed it was Lucian.

"I got ya." Terrance grabbed one of Lucian's arms and helped guide him.

"Okay, Lucian, what's our next step?" Mira asked.

"We're looking for a set of doors. They'll probably have something written on them that says 'maintenance only.'"

Mira looked around. This had to have been an old warehouse or something. She made out the shapes of boxes, and by the musty smell knew the place had a heavy coat of dust. At her feet, she nearly slipped on papers strewn about the floor. "Careful where you step," she warned, and continued in further. At the far end she spied a couple of sets of doors. "This way," she said, and headed toward a pair that had small windows in them. A white sign proclaimed in red letters *Authorized Personnel Only*.

"I think I found it," Mira called over to the group. She pushed through the doors, and blew out a sigh of relief when no more alarms sounded.

"What do you see?" Lucian asked nervously.

Peering into the darkness, she tried to make sense of what she was seeing. "Looks like a long hallway with doors everywhere," Mira called back.

"Great!" The relief in Lucian's voice was clear. "Okay, now look for ones marked 'stairs.'"

"Stay close," Mira said, and slowly, she made her way down the hallway, stopping every few feet to check for signs and listen for any sound of guards.

When she found a door marked *stairs*, Mira pushed it open. Alarm bells began to blare. Red lights flashed, bathing the hall and stairwell in crimson light.

Mira covered her ears against the shrill sound. "Make it stop!"

Lucian sprang to action. On the outside of the door was a security panel. He began tapping in various codes. When one appeared not to work, he tried another, and another. "They must have deactivated some of my codes," Lucian shouted, as if anyone could actually hear him over the noise.

Sensitive as her ears were, the noise was painfully piercing. She could hear nothing else except for the shrill siren.

"Let me try one more," Lucian, said though he was sure no one could hear him. He frantically tapped in a long ten-digit code.

Silence fell like a wet blanket over the group, drowning out the shrill call of the alarm. The lights stopped flashing, but the red glow remained.

"What happened?" Mira found herself yelling over the ringing of her ears.

"Security protocols. All entrances and exits to classified areas were armed with alarm systems. I thought since these buildings were old and no longer in use, their alarms might have been deactivated. I was wrong."

"So, does that mean your codes work?" Mira asked.

"Mine didn't, but I have a few others memorized." Lucian said with a proud smile. "We changed codes so often that I needed to have a few backups on hand in case I couldn't remember my own personal one. Comes in handy every now and again."

The ringing began to subside, and Mira was better able to control the volume of her voice. "Let's just hope that your codes will still be good when we get to the prison cells."

"And we'll have to move double time. They'll be on to us now that this alarm has gone off." Lucian said.

CHAPTER EIGHT

T hough the red lighted hallways meant almost certainly
that the group were being watched and would soon be
attacked, they were thankful to not have to stumble around in the
dark anymore.

Lower and lower they traveled, down shaky metal stairwells
and into the depths of the city's infrastructure. When they had
gone as low as they could, Lucian guided them toward a set of
blue double doors. Beyond them was a hallway Mira recognized.
She been so turned around the first time she'd been there; but
now, standing in that hallway again, she recognized the place
where she'd first set eyes on Lucian. How close she'd been to
freedom then! If she'd only known.

"From here on out, there will surely be guards. And cameras," Lucian said.

"Forget the cameras, they'll already know we're here. Stealth
is no longer the goal; now we need deadly speed. We need to get
to the prison level and release my friends," Mira said. "Once we
do that, we'll be able to battle our way out."

"Agreed. The wolves will need to take up the lead and rear.
The handlers will have UV weaponry," Lucian reminded her.

Mira hissed involuntarily at the mention of the torches. She
knew their sting all too well. "Lead the way."

Lucian led the charge down the hallways. The first guard they ran into didn't know what had hit him. The wolves were quick and merciless in their attack, snapping the young man's neck before he had the idea that anyone was behind him.

The next guard was not so lucky. He saw the cadre charging him and tried to raise his weapon in time, but there was no hope.

When they reached the prison level and opened the door, bright white light flooded Mira's vision, blinding her. Hissing in pain, she turned away from the light. Alarms had already been raised and every cell was flooded with overhead UV lighting. The cacophony of screams and moans from the imprisoned vampires was so loud it overwhelmed the alarms. She couldn't see them, but Mira knew they were all writhing in pain, burning, screaming for mercy.

"Do something!" Mira shrieked, unable to enter the doorway. She clutched at her face, trying to shield her eyes.

"I'm on it," Lucian yelled.

Strong warm arms enveloped Mira, blocking her body from much of the burning light. "Relax. I've got you." Stryker's tone was calm and reassuring. "You two, stay with the human!"

Mira couldn't say anything; the pain was tremendous. Any small bit of skin exposed singed and burned. She tried to make herself as small as she could, hiding in the shadow of Stryker's strong body, thankful for his immunity to the light and his size.

It felt like an eternity, but when the alarms finally hushed, the sudden silence was just as deafening as the screams had been. A few whimpers broke the silence, and then groans and grunts began to reach Mira's ears as vampires rose up in their cells.

"Blood. They'll need it. Immediately." Fearful urgency tainted her voice. "Tell Lucian to open the ration stores. The vampires when released will be a feral as dogs after what they just went through."

"Are you okay? Can you move?" Stryker asked.

"I'm fine, but he won't be if he releases their cages before opening up the stores of rations. Go!"

Stryker disappeared quickly. Mira blinked away the sting in her eyes and refocused through the new darkness. Footsteps, lots of them behind her, set her on edge. She knew the humans would be coming, but had hoped for a few minutes to explain to her vampire kindred what was going on before they were invaded.

Anxiously she turned and saw the hoard of guards flooding through the doorway behind her. Trapped, she was the only thing blocking their way into the prison floor.

"We've got company." She barely got the words out before the lights hit her square in the face. UV torches: painful blasts of hot light. Shrieking in pain, Mira crumpled to the ground again. For all her strength, she was powerless being assaulted by so many lights at once.

A wolf snarled and something dark leapt over her. Then another shape came around her side. Guns went off and men screamed. Mira was caught up in the bodies that pushed into her like a tide against the seashore. From both sides they came at her, crashing together in a loud roar. The painful lights disappeared. Free from their blinding beams, Mira sprang into action. Wolves along with the recently freed vampires were already deeply entrenched in the fight. Blood sprayed into the air, speckling her face.

Mira found herself at a loss as to whom she could attack. All around her was a swarming mass of bodies, some dismembered, some still writhing in pain. All of her kind, the others who'd been imprisoned for so long, were feasting on the fallen soldiers. As gruesome as the scene before her was, she'd not deny her fellow inmates the pleasure of this well-earned meal, and found herself smiling as she watched them in action. Even the wolves looked to be enjoying taking down soldiers as they attempted to file into the room.

Lucian cautiously approached her from behind. She felt his trembling hand on her shoulder before she turned.

"You did it!" Mira's eyes glinted with bloodlust, but she tried to rein it in for his sake.

The look on Lucian's face was not a happy one. "So much death."

"This is war. It's what happens." Mira shrugged. For someone accustomed to seeing her kind slaughtering each other in the arena while he ate his steak and potatoes, he was a little too squeamish about it now.

"But those soldiers… humans…"

"Would just as easily kill me, them, and you." He might have been on her side, but he was still human. Seeing his own kind being killed was clearly affecting him more than he wanted to say. She could see it in the faraway look and hear the hesitation in his voice.

"Needless deaths." Lucian's voice was almost a whisper.

"Once we change things, hopefully there will be no more need of senseless deaths," Mira said, and truly meant it. Though the smell of fresh blood tempted her, she was sick of death.

Lucian snorted. "Don't put so much faith in humanity."

"I don't; nor do I put my faith in my own kind. But I have hope."

His eyebrow quirked up and he finally met her eyes dead on. "You constantly surprise me."

"How so?"

"You are surprisingly softhearted, for a vampire."

"And then you had to go ruin the moment with a statement like that," Mira shot at Lucian. Soft… there was nothing soft about her.

Behind them, the sounds of the massacre were diminishing. Mira felt the weight of eyes falling on her, and more importantly, on Lucian. She turned swiftly and pulled him behind her. Acting as his shield, she met the icy stare of Tegan, leading the pack of rabid vampires. The hulking beast of a man lumbered toward her. Hunger and rage filling his cold eyes. Years of pent-up aggression needing to be slaked.

"If you're not going to partake, at least share..." Thick with fresh blood, Tegan's voice carried a wicked note to it. One that promised danger.

Caught between two worlds, Mira understood Tegan's murderous glares at her human friend, their former jailer. But she'd not let him touch a hair on Lucian's head. "No one is partaking in this one." Mira matched his tone, promising more than just danger to him if he tried anything.

"Look who's gone all soft for her human patron. Finally get a little action, and now look at you." His mocking hit a nerve. She'd be lying if she said she wasn't tempted to entertain his unasked challenge, but they had better things to do than fight among themselves.

"If it weren't for him, you wouldn't be out here. No one touches this human. Got it?"

"Human lover," Tegan spat. Vampires behind him cheered as if it had been a rallying call.

Baring her teeth, she snarled, "Back off, Tegan. Last warning."

The two wolves, Rob and Terrance, were instantly at Mira's side. Ears pinned back and growling, they were on high alert. The hairs on the back of the wolves' necks almost stood straight up. Stryker pushed his way through the crowd, fists balled up so tight he was shaking with anticipation.

Hand twitching a the hilt of her short sword, Mira stared deep into Tegan's eyes. "We're prepared for a fight, Tegan. Back down now and we can talk this out. Remember, I'm not your enemy."

"Call your dogs off! This is bullshit." Tegan stamped his foot like a child. "We're free now. Time to make our captors pay."

"We will. But he's not one of them," Mira said, her tone still warning, but calming a bit. "He's under my protection and the protection of the Otherkin."

"He's Elite. He's a Regent!" Tegan lunged forward and tried to push Mira aside. "Ruler of this city. The one who was our jailer!"

Ready for him, Mira was a stone wall, unmoving, even with the full weight of him pushing against her. "He *was*, Tegan! Not anymore." She hoped he would get the picture, but Tegan had always been a bit thick in the head.

Stryker twitched, ready to fight at her side. A low rumbling growl rolled up his chest. But he made no move to intercede yet.

The other vampires fanned out around them as best they could in the corridor. None stepped forward to issue a challenge. Glancing quickly into the crowd, she hoped to see George, but didn't have time to have a good look, not with Tegan's threatening glare directed at her. Despite the fact they all were warriors, she got the impression that Tegan was the acting Alpha in this group, and she'd have to knock him down from his throne if she hoped to get anyone else to listen.

Mira turned to Stryker. "If he wants a fight, so be it. But this fight is between me and him."

Lucian, without prompting, sidestepped behind Stryker. The two wolves growled and bared their teeth at the vampires encircling them, but made no move.

Mira narrowed her eyes at Tegan, daring him to do something stupid.

"You'd really fight one of your own, over this human?" Tegan spat in her face.

A feral growl rumbled out of Mira's throat as she wiped the spittle from her eyes.

Clearly satisfied he'd shamed her, Tegan stepped closer, invading her space and smiling as he looked down his nose at her.

That would be the last time he pulled a stunt like that. Moving with all her vampiric speed, Mira had his balls in her right hand, and squeezed, digging her nails into the soft yielding flesh. "Try a stunt like that again and I rip them off."

His head came down hard against hers. Two wrecking balls colliding with a loud crack; the impact stunned them both, but Mira held firm to her prize, jerking them a little as she recovered.

"Final warning, Tegan. Submit, or become a eunuch the hard way."

More brawn than brains, he still held to his rage. Stepping into Mira, he threw his arms around her and squeezed.

Her head squashed against his shoulder, Mira had little room to move, but she would not let go. Rather than drop her leverage and squirm away, she found an open bit of flesh and bit down. Vampire blood was a far superior source of replenishment, and after her light bath a few moments earlier, she needed it. Tegan howled and tried to back away, but realized she was still in control of his balls. He beat against her back with his fists, and she responded by digging her teeth into his shoulder while tightening her grip on his most sensitive bits. The absurdity of their embrace must have been a sight, but no one surrounding them made a sound.

Grumbling with aggravation, Tegan released her. "Fine! Have your human. Just let me go!"

Mira released him and stepped back, wiping the blood from her mouth. "He's not just any human. He risked his life to free me, and we risked everything together to free you. Not all humans are our enemies, but the ones that are, I promise you, we will repay for the atrocities done to our kind." Mira held out her hand in friendship to Tegan. "Trust me. He's not our enemy."

He looked at her suspiciously for a moment.

"Remember what I said to you before I was dragged from the arena? Someday it will be your turn to do something… Now's that time."

Recognition and understanding sparked in his eyes, but he still hesitated before taking her offered hand. "What's your plan?"

Tegan, though an ass, had always been a good fighter. And by all appearances, he was the Alpha in this group of vampires. None of the others had stepped up to her yet. So, Mira was glad to have Tegan on her side. "We form an army."

"To do what, exactly?" he asked.

"Take down the Magistrate, with our new friends, the Otherkin."

"You mean these dogs?"

"Careful, Tegan."

The wolves growled. Stryker stepped in closer.

"The wolves are part but not all of the Otherkin society. Tegan… Sanctuary is real. And, we can all go there." Mira addressed the rest of the vampires. "All we have to do is help them fight back. Are you with me?"

CHAPTER NINE

A caramel-skinned vampire limped his way to the front of the crowd. His bald head gave him away before Mira could see his face. She'd been worried she hadn't seen him, hoping something had not happened while she was away. He looked a little more worn than she remembered. He limped slowly, his leg trickling blood without stopping.

George pushed his way to the front of the crowd. He met Mira's eyes and his own began to water as a smile of pure joy bloomed across his face. "You always said you'd escape. I never believed before – but look at me now, eating crow. I'm not about to do it again. You say you can wage a war and win the hearts of our enemies... I'll believe it. Whatever you need from me, I'll do."

She rushed to him, pulling his large frame into her arms.

"What happened to you? Are you okay?"

"Just a flesh wound..."

"Liar. Let me take a look at it." She bent down to inspect it. A shard of metal jutted out from the wound, and the skin was refusing to heal around it. "Silver-coated. Someone get me something to pull this out."

She pushed George to the ground and ripped open his pant leg to get a better look at the wound. The metal was embedded deeper than she could get with her nails. She needed tweezers or something with a little more precision and reach. No one had moved at her first request for help, so she upped the volume. "Help your fellow gladiator, you spineless bastards. No wonder the humans treat you as savages!"

That got their attention. She didn't see who, but someone handed her a pair of tweezers and a few rags to soak up the blood. "This is going to hurt a little." That was all the warning she gave before diving into the wound to fish out the metal preventing his wound from healing. Discomfort played across George's face, but to his credit, he did not whine or complain. He hissed and panted while she worked.

The piece was larger than she'd thought initially, but as soon as she pulled it out, George's leg began to heal, skin knitting back together as if it had never been cut. She held out her wrist. "Take my blood to help."

George whispered a thank you and bit into her offered wrist.

She winced as his teeth pierced her flesh and turned away to address the others. "If you will not help one of your own, you might as well put yourself back in those cells, because that is where you'll eventually end up. You're still outnumbered by the humans. That's how they have the advantage. And they'll always have that advantage so long as you act alone…"

Tegan's threatening stance relaxed, but he had not agreed to join them; at least not yet. "So we have to fight for the Otherkin? Those are your terms?"

"I offer no formal terms." Mira had to hold back the snicker. She was no diplomat come to discuss a treaty. The though alone was absurd. "I'm asking you to join us on this campaign. We want to end the humans' treatment of our kind. And we do that by joining forces. They will see we are a force to be reckoned with, no longer slaves."

"We are a force to be reckoned with. And we will use that force to wreck this city!" Tegan spoke to the crowd, rallying them with his confidence.

They roared in agreement around him.

She was losing ground quickly. Of course they wanted revenge. Who would blame them for that? But she needed to focus it if she hoped to rally them to her cause. Mira shouted above the crowds roar. "Yes... you could wreck this city. You could raze it to the ground. But where is the satisfaction in killing innocents? It's the Elites who enslave us. It is the magistrates and regents who order our deaths. Our fight is with them, not the general populace. Join us and we will make them pay."

Surprisingly, Lucian decided to chime in. He stepped out from behind Stryker. "Why not capture the Magistrate and bring him back to the Otherkin as a prize?"

"That might not be too bad an idea." Mira glanced back at Lucian. "Take out the head of the government and bring him up before the Otherkin council."

Lucian nodded, but there was hesitation in his eyes. "That might work. Without their leader though, the local regents would take charge. We would—"

"It takes time to re-establish leadership," Mira interrupted. "What if we were able to put the Magistrate and his crimes on public display? Help change public opinion before anything rash happens. Revenge is best when it is made public." She turned back towards Tegan. "That's what you want, right, revenge in its purest form?"

Now it was Stryker's time to speak up. "Our orders were clear. Free the vampires and bring them back to join the army."

She shot him a warning glare and leaned in, whispering low. "You will still have your army, but I have to convince them our ideals are aligned. Besides, what better than an army that never needs to be used?"

"That's not for us to decide," Stryker said.

"Right now, it is. Keep quiet. These are my people to deal with." Her tone brooked no argument and thankfully, the wolf did not press further. Mira turned back to Tegan. "Well, I think no matter which way we go, if the Magistrate is still here, we should go after him."

"And you think working together as a team will make us want to join you?" Tegan said.

"Yeah. I do," she shot back at him, and then addressed the crowd. "Your chances are better with us than alone. Let's say you exact your revenge. What happens next? Daylight comes, and now you're in a hostile city, hoping to wait out the day. Or, you get with the program, get some revenge, and earn a place in Sanctuary with people just like us."

A collective rumble of agreement came from the crowd.

"So, let's grab the Magistrate, and take him back to the Council."

"As long as it doesn't take too long, yes, let's get him," Stryker agreed.

"Well? You with us?" Mira looked at Tegan.

"We'll help get the Magistrate. No promises on the whole army part. You didn't just free us to make us slaves to someone else's whims."

"No one is a slave. Do what you like. I'm finished talking. Let's go."

"No promises," Tegan repeated, looking back over his shoulder to the others surrounding him. "We'll help get the Magistrate and anyone else we kill along the way."

"Once we have him, we'll rendezvous with the Otherkin. Decide then if you want to continue," Mira said.

"This will need to be a targeted attack," Lucian interjected. "We're not aiming for civilians, just the Elites along the way. Those who put you in those cages. We want to make an example of them, but not hurt those who are innocent."

"No human is innocent. Have you seen the way they cheer for our deaths in the arena?" Tegan snarled.

They were going round in circles, and Mira was quickly losing patience. Talk was something diplomats did. She was a warrior. She was ready to get up and see some action. "They don't know any better. They were raised to think we are savages." She couldn't believe the words escaped her lips, and yet, she still felt the need to say it in defense of the screaming masses.

"That's no excuse," Tegan shot back.

"It's not a good excuse," she agreed, "but it is the truth. They don't believe we are thinking and feeling creatures, so they don't feel the sympathy they should for our lives and deaths." Mira said matter-of-factly. "We have to show them that all they have learned is wrong."

"Yes. The rest of the human population is clueless. Show them you're not a threat to them, only to those who have spread the lies about your kind," Lucian said

"Prove to the humans that we are not just savages," Mira challenged.

"And you think by killing their leaders that the rest of the human population is going to fall in line?" Tegan laughed. "You're insane."

"It's not a perfect plan, but yeah, by targeting our attack we show them we're not mindless killers. Lucian here will be our envoy when the dust clears to help smooth the rest of the way," Mira said.

Tegan and a few other vampires laughed almost hysterically. "No humans will ever trust our kind or treat us with any respect."

George stood, his leg almost completely healed now. "If Mira says she's going to do something, she will. I have complete faith in her. She'll make this plan work."

"What say the rest of you?" Mira looked around the crowd. "Will you stand with me and work towards peace, or will you mindlessly kill every human you can until they find a way to imprison you again?"

Murmurs swept through the space. Mira could tell not all were convinced she could do what she claimed. The fact of the matter was, she wasn't truly convinced either, but they had to do something. Things could not continue the way they had. Between human, vampire, and Otherkin, there was too much at stake. Peace, even a tenuous one, was better than what they had now.

Tegan spoke up as representative of the mass. "We'll fight our way out of the city with you, and help you take out the Magistrate, but we make no promises beyond that."

"I guess I'll have to take that, for now." Mira said. "Lucian will lead the way. Our next target will be the capital building."

"Sounds tasty," Tegan said.

"Only take out the Elites. The rest of the humans are to be left alive. Incapacitate them only if necessary; do not kill them. Spill none of their blood!"

"I don't take orders from humans anymore," Tegan spat at Lucian.

Lucian appeared shaken being threatened by the larger vampire, but he didn't back down. "If you want this to work, you're going to need to work with me, not against me."

Seeing Lucian confident and even a little arrogant made her smile. If only he weren't human...

"What he said goes." Mira added further weight to Lucian's order. "We're not on a blind massacre. Now you either do as we ask, or I'll put you on your ass faster than I did in the arena."

George flashed her his brilliant smile. "I got your back, lady!"

Having his support warmed her heart, but she needed to get the rest on board, and they all seemed content with Tegan as their spokesperson.

Tegan muttered something under his breath then waved his hand as if to say, "Lead the way."

Mira let out a sigh of relief. She knew the animosity between them wasn't over, but for the moment, they were on the same team. "Where to?" she asked Lucian.

CHAPTER TEN

L ucian led them down a series of hallways, all of them lit by red blinking lights accompanied by sirens blaring. There was no point in trying to shut them down now. They needed to get to the capitol building and find the Magistrate before he was whisked off to some safe and undisclosed location.

Every twist, every turn, each new corridor they traveled down brought on a new series of soldiers. Despite Mira's order to try to leave humans alive, she knew the soldiers were dead before she rounded the next corner. Minor casualties, she told herself, as if it might be a comfort. They were all part of the problem as it was, armed with UV torches and fully intent on using them. It was the hearts and minds of the normal folk that she needed to sway.

On they went, traveling as fast as they could, until they found an underground corridor with a large instrument panel next to it.

"This one should take us straight to the capitol. It's how I came down to find you that first day." Lucian said to Mira. "Triple locked, and the door handles are silver coated. If the wrong code is entered, silver nitrate will release from above."

"A bit of overkill, don't you think?" Mira asked.

"When you're dealing with half-starved and lethally trained vampire prisoners... no."

She frowned. Clearly, he hadn't heard the sarcasm in her tone. "Can you open it?"

Lucian stared intently at the instrument panel, studying its every button and light. He waved a hand behind him as if to say, "Quiet."

Mira took the hint. She turned back to the crowd of vampires and wolves who'd been following in her wake. "Watch our backs. Going to be a few minutes here."

George found his way in front of the crowd again. He pulled Mira in to an unexpected hug. "Sorry. I just had to! All those years separated by the bars in our cell. You always had it rough. You need this more than anyone." He squeezed her so tight she felt the air being pushed out of her lungs.

"Not the time nor the place, George." Mira choked on her breath. She wasn't the hugging type, no matter who it was on the other end of the squeeze, but somehow, she didn't mind too much when it came from George. He'd saved her so many times from the effects of starvation. Shared the last of his rations, and his wisdom. If any vampire out there could be considered kin, he certainly could.

"Never is the time and never will be the place. Quit complaining. You can knock me on my ass if you want, but I have thirty years' worth of hugs to give you."

"Okay, I give!" Half choking and half laughing, Mira beat her fists into his back. "Let me go."

George released her and met her eyes with a smile so wide she felt his face might split in two. "Now I can die a happy man."

"No one is going to die today... well, no vampire. But don't get your hopes up. We still have a long way to go."

"Always the optimist." Stryker joined Mira. He held a hand out to George. "I've had the pleasure of her positivity for the better part of a week now."

"Try thirty years…" George chuckled. He grabbed Stryker's hand and introduced himself. With a little wink, he whispered to Mira. "I approve."

Warmth rushed to her cheeks. She turned away to hide the blush. What was George implying, and how could he even suggest…?

"I think she likes you, Stryker," George teased.

Before she could respond with an angry threat to both of their manhoods, Lucian shouted, "Got it!"

Thankful to have the change in subject, Mira rushed over to Lucian.

"I think I can override the security protocols and get my code to work. Just in case it doesn't, though, you might want to have everyone stand back ten or so feet."

Mira turned. "Step back a bit," she ordered.

"Good! When we get inside, things might get crazy," Lucian warned. "No doubt the Magistrate has been alerted. He may already be en route to a safe home. But any and all guards will be waiting and ready with orders to kill."

"No worse than what we have already encountered." Mira shrugged.

"That remains to be seen. The Magistrate will be heavily guarded. Just be prepared for anything," Lucian said.

"Lead the way."

In they went, Mira expecting a hoard of guards to greet her. She was surprised instead by the complete lack of any sign of human inhabitants. There was barely a trace of human smell in the sterile white corridor.

"You said prepare for anything… how about nothing?" she said, disappointed.

"He's already gone," Lucian confirmed. "But we might be able to pick up a trail. This way." He took off in a sprint.

They followed behind, winding through ever more maze-like hallways. Mira was sure she'd never be able to find her way out again as many times as they had twisted, turned, and gone up and down various levels of stairs.

Suddenly, Stryker stopped and sniffed at the air. "I smell something. This way." He darted through a set of doors that opened into a cavernous room not unlike the cave where the Otherkin stored their collected transport vehicles. And there, in the center, a transport sat. One that looked like the VT Curtis had so lovingly inspected back in Caldera Grove. Its engines rumbled as they began to power up, but its hatch door still remained open.

As soon as Mira entered the room, the plane began to empty of its passengers. At least two dozen men dressed in black poured from the small hatch door, opening fire as they fanned out around the flying transport.

Bullets ricocheted off the walls. Lights from the UV torches flashed in the vampires' direction.

"Kill all but the Elites," Mira bellowed over the noise, and blindly charged forward.

Bullets raced through her skin, stinging and searing her flesh as they passed through her, but she was undeterred in her mission. Grabbing the closest soldier she could reach, she snapped his neck and dropped his body to the ground. Another soldier was on her before she could turn around. The butt of his rifle poked her in the back and he let a few rounds go. She shrieked with pain and twisted around, knocking the weapon from his hand while simultaneously snatching him by the neck. He would not be allowed to die so quickly. She needed his blood to heal and needed him to feel some of the pain he'd just inflicted on her. Baring her teeth she sank them into his hot flesh.

Blood had never tasted so good, but she had no time to indulge. Ripping out his throat as she pulled away, Mira left the soldier to bleed out and die at her feet while she moved on to the next. The hanger was a mess of blood and carnage as all the vampires took to feasting on their prey. The aircraft was beginning to move. Passengers or crew – Mira wasn't exactly sure which they were – began to pull up the hatch door, attempting to close it before anyone else could get onboard.

Stryker was one step ahead of Mira, jumping to catch the door before it sealed shut. He grabbed and pulled with all his might, slamming it back to the ground. A human fell out with the door, but rather than attack Mira, he scrambled up and ran the other way. Mira didn't give chase, knowing someone else would take care of him.

The hanger filled with a horrible metallic screeching as the vertical transport dragged the heavy door while it taxied around the space.

"Get onboard, quick!" Stryker said, holding the door open, as the transport dragged him behind it.

Mira jumped up the small stairs built into the door frame and climbed into the cabin.

Inside she met with the barrel of a gun held in the shaky hands of the Magistrate. "I'll blow that pretty face of yours right off," he said.

"I'll heal." Mira slapped the gun from his hand as if it were a toy.

The Magistrate jumped backwards in fear.

Something hard came crashing down on Mira's head. It hurt, but did nothing more than annoy her. She turned to find another man, one she'd never seen before, holding a suitcase in his hands.

"Did you think that would work?" Mira said with annoyance.

Jaw agape, the man stood dumbfounded and shaking.

"Cut the engines and stop this plane now before I kill you all," Mira ordered.

"You're going to kill us anyway," the Magistrate said.

"Not yet. But if you don't do as I ask, I most certainly will... Slowly and very painfully." Mira licked her fangs. "Your call."

"I could just take off and let the sun bake you while we fly." The Magistrate stood and regained some of his cocky attitude.

"Empty threat. Sunrise isn't for a few more hours. Besides, you'd never make it past the hanger door, and there's a hungry band of vampires ready and willing to feast on your flabby flesh. I'm the only thing preventing that at the moment."

Curiosity seemed to overtake the Magistrate's apparent fear. He suddenly stopped trembling. "Why?"

"I have my reasons. But none of them include patience. Cut the engines now, or I'll kill you myself."

The Magistrate nodded to his shaking friend. The man turned and disappeared into the cockpit. A moment later, the aircraft came to a sudden stop.

"Smart man. Now move your lard ass and do exactly as I say." Suppressing a sneer at his horrid scent, she walked behind him, seized his wrist, and jerked his arm nearly straight up his back. The Magistrate hissed in pain but was smart enough not to fight back.

"Let's go." Mira nudged him forward.

She emerged from the transport holding the Magistrate's arms behind his back.

Below them, waiting patiently on the ground, eyes filled with bloodlust, were her vampire allies. All of them looked moments from pouncing. She tightened her grip on the Magistrate's arm and glared down at the hungry mass. "We have what we came here for!" Her voice was loud, poised, and carried an authority that they dared not oppose. "Let's take him back to the Otherkin and collect our reward.... Sanctuary!"

She pushed him forward, and he slowly stepped down toward the mass of vampires and other creatures cheering below.

"Remember – no one is to harm him. We'll take him to the Otherkin leaders at the rendezvous point. Is this clear?" Though she had already warned them enough, one more time wouldn't hurt.

The crowd grumbled in agreement. Mira really hadn't expected more than that. She was asking so much of them. And, to their credit, the vampires were all restraining themselves better than she'd expected.

"And how do you propose we get there?" Tegan asked.

"We walk out the front door. We have their Magistrate," Mira said. "And the Regent too." She nodded at Lucian.

"We're not walking the entire way," Tegan scoffed.

"No, just to the city center to show them we have their leader. Then, we can steal some transports and make our way out in style."

"Good, because for a second there I thought you forgot what time it was."

Mira had forgotten, but didn't want to let on. "No, of course not. We still have a few hours, but we do need to make a good show before we go."

Stryker, standing at Lucian's side, grabbed the former Regent's arm and twisted it behind his back. "Ready to transport the prisoners."

Lucian grunted in pain, turning an angry eye to the wolfman.

Stryker said nothing, all the while looking as if he were suppressing a smile. Mira was certain he was enjoying manhandling her human friend, but there was no time to worry about it now. They had more important things to deal with.

"Stick together, Move out. And remember... no unnecessary deaths!"

"As soon as we get outside, I'll send word of our victory," Stryker promised.

CHAPTER ELEVEN

J ay, the little bird shifter, flitted around them as they proudly emerged from the capitol building. Mira and Stryker took the lead, holding their prisoners for all the city to see. The rest of their band of vampires and shifters casually strolled behind them.

The capitol building might have been emptied of soldiers, but the streets were still alive with humans, thanks to all the sirens that had been going on for hours. To the humans, the sight of their leaders being escorted by savages must have been a truly horrific sight.

Shrieks and screams of fear accompanied many a human running in the opposite direction from their parade through the city streets, but no one tried to stop their march toward the city gate.

"Let our leaders know we are returning with the Magistrate," Stryker said to the little brown bird. "We'll take a transport to rendezvous with them shortly."

Jay trilled something softly and disappeared into the sky.

"I have a working transport… we really don't need to parade me through the streets." Magistrate Mathias's arrogance had not left him despite being a prisoner. He huffed and struggled to keep the pace. Mira doubted he'd ever walked this far in his life. Good. He could use a little exercise, the overstuffed pig.

"We'll walk to the city center, to show the rest of the humans you are alive, well, and under our control," she barked at him, shoving him a little harder to quicken his pace.

Though it was difficult, Mira tried to make eye contact with every human they passed by. She wanted them to see that rather than slaughter their leader, she and the rest of the vampires were peacefully walking away with him, driving home the subtle but very important message.

Most humans would not give her a second look, running scared the moment the mass of vampires came anywhere near them. One human, however, did meet her gaze.

Olivia Preston clip-clopped her way toward the parade, in her way-too-high heels, seemingly unafraid. "The prodigal vampire returns to wage war on the city. You always were a troublemaker."

"And you always had less sense than you should," Mira responded. "Walk away now, and I'll leave you with your life. Which is far more than you deserve for the way you and your family treated me."

"You want to complain of your treatment… do you know what you cost me?"

Mira's ability to rein in her temper was at its limit. "Final warning."

"You lost me everything! Your little stunt in the arena. You bankrupted me…my family…"

"What family? You've never worn a ring on that finger. Don't pretend."

"Details… what does it matter now? I'm ruined. My name is worthless."

"At least you had something to lose."

"You want me to deal with her?" George stepped in and put a calm hand on Mira's trembling arm as the rage within her threatened to bubble over.

"No. I will. Hold him." She pushed the Magistrate into George's arms. "You." She addressed her former owner. "Want to know what it is to truly lose it all? Fine." Baring her teeth, she sank them into the hot flesh of Olivia's neck. Oh, how she'd dreamed of this day! Fantasized about it for years. Draining the life out of that pampered princess. Feeling her limbs grow weak. Hearing the slowing thump of her heart as her blood pressure plummeted. A dream come true now that she had the fading human growing limp in her arms.

But death was simply too good a fate for her. Just as Olivia's heart slowed and almost stilled, Mira pulled away. "Now you can truly know what it means to be on the bottom. To have lost it all." She bit into her wrist and forced the bleeding wound over Olivia's mouth. Though she was nearly unconscious, Olivia swallowed instinctively. Mira let her drink until strength came back into her limbs and she clung to Mira for support. Once Mira felt those polished nails digging into her skin, she dropped Olivia to the ground.

Wide unfocused eyes met hers. Olivia was beginning to change. Mira spat in her former owner's face. "Now you'll truly understand. May luck be on your side." Mira looked back at the rest of her group, meeting each pair of questioning eyes with determination. "Leave Olivia here," she ordered. "If she survives the night, she can fend off the handlers and soldiers alone."

Awestruck, the other vampires looked at Mira as if they'd never truly seen her before. No one dared question her. At that moment, she knew she'd taken leadership of the group. She was the alpha now. She was their leader, their general, and had earned their respect.

"Remind me never to piss you off," George said hesitantly. "Damn… you're evil…. In the best way."

"Evil is all about perspective. She got what was coming to her." Mira took hold of the Magistrate again and led the march onward toward the city center. The last time she'd been in that place, they'd been nailing her down to a table as an offering to the sun, punishment of the worst kind for a vampire. Death by sunburn. This time, she was there to make a different example. She and her kind were no longer slaves.

"Gather round!" she called. When they reached the city center, Tables for burning vampires were still set out in the city square. A small shudder rolled its way down her back as she remembered the sensation of the wood at her back and the spikes in her wrist. Deep down she felt a little crazy, fighting for an end to this battle between human and Otherkin, but another more savage part of her wanted the same revenge her brethren did. So many atrocities had been visited upon her kind. So many needless deaths.

But more death was just not the answer, angry as she was about it all.

"You okay?" George placed a comforting hand on her back.

She didn't mean to jump, but the unfamiliar gesture caught her off guard. "Fine. Just anticipating some resistance," she lied.

None of the humans around were willing to show themselves, but Mira felt the weight of their scrutinizing eyes on her.

"We mean you no harm," she called out to any who might hear. The audacity of her words gave her pause. How could she prove that when she was holding their leader captive? "You've been lied to all these years. People in power have deceived you. We are here to bring out the truth and forge a new peace."

It all sounded good in her head. Even her voice sounded sympathetic, a first for her, but still none of the humans lurking around were willing to come out.

Mira nudged the Magistrate forward. "Say something to them."

He turned a cold eye on her. "You want me to speak for you? Are you mad?"

"Clearly... Just do it. Tell them to come; see we have not harmed you."

"No. You want to win them over. Do it on your own."

The desire to rip open his throat was more prevalent than ever. If not for his stench, she might have just given in and taken him. But that wouldn't have helped their situation either. She was trying to show good will and effect change, not start an all-out bloody war.

Mira turned to Stryker. "Call in the transport. We'll just have to skip the meet and greet."

He nodded and whistled to his wolves. The two disappeared into the crowd of vampires.

In the eerie silence of waiting, Mira caught the quirk of Magistrate's lip. If she didn't know better, she'd have thought he was smiling, but that couldn't be the case... or could it?

"What's so amusing?" she asked.

"Nothing." He was lying, and she knew it.

"Look to the shadows. Something isn't right!" Mira ordered.

Lights flickered on around her. Beams of pure searing heat. She should have expected as much, but was not prepared for it. Shock rippled through the crowd. Vampires ducked and covered their eyes against the burn. The Magistrate took that moment to squirm from Mira's grip, but she did not let him get far. His hefty body made for a perfect shield, at least from the front. She gripped him tightly with both hands, digging her nails into his puffy shoulders. "Not so fast."

Moans and wails merged with a battle cry from an oncoming human hoard. Hundreds of men and women, all bearing the hammer and stake shield on their uniforms, ran into the mass like waves rushing upon the shore.

Lights flashed, blood splattered, and cries of pain broke through the shouting and were quickly silenced.

"Is this really what you want? Send as many men in as you can, Magistrate, we are immortal. Your lights will not last forever." It was all Mira could do not to rip the man's throat out herself, but she knew he was better for the cause alive than dead. That was the only reason she hadn't already snapped his puffy neck.

Despite his precarious position, he let out a cackle. "Our lights will last well beyond dawn, and where will your vampires be then?"

"You think it's only vampires out there for you to fear? I know you know better than that." She was banking on it. "Look there.... You see that one doesn't flinch from your lights. And there... and there..." She pointed to each wolf, hoping that three would be enough to satisfy his fears. He didn't need to know they were the only ones she'd brought.

He remained silent, but the hard bob of his Adam's apple as he gulped down fear told her all she needed to know.

"That's what I thought." She bent down and whispered slowly in his ear. "Otherkin aren't afraid of the light."

Mira had been so focused on the Magistrate she'd failed to notice someone coming up behind her. As the scent of human wafted to her nose, a heavy brick hit the backside of her head. Stars danced in her vision before the world began to spin. Holding on as best she could to reality, Mira fought the pull of unconsciousness. She couldn't let the Magistrate get away. Tightening her grip, she dug her nails into his skin, breaking it and sending blood rushing to the surface to meet her fingers.

The Magistrate's painful moan sounded as if it were coming from underwater.

Head aching and vision darkening, Mira turned to see who'd struck her. A hand cocked back, ready to strike, hovered above her. The human it belonged to was a stranger, but he had the determined look of a handler in his eyes.

"Drop him." The order was loud, but the ringing in Mira's ears made it hard for her to hear clearly.

"I'd rather kill him and you," she slurred, fighting past the pain to stay in reality.

"Last warning, leech."

She really despised that name, but if he wanted to play that way, she'd let him. Mira threw her head forward, smashing into the Magistrate. He fell unconscious from the blow, and Mira felt confident enough to drop his limp body for the moment. When she turned back to face her opponent, blaring light seared her skin.

"I'm sick of these damned lights!" she shouted. Too much pain had overwhelmed her senses, and she was beyond feeling. In the space of a heartbeat, she swiped the weapon away and pulled the man in close. "You people have pushed me too far..." All the years she had wanted to do this: take a handler and drain him slowly, painfully. Just the thought of it brought a smile to her face.

"Let me go... Drop me... Stop!" Fear killed the authority in the handler's voice. Desperation filled his eyes, but Mira could no longer care. He wasn't worth saving. He'd never live in peace with vampires... at least, that was her justification as she sank her teeth deep into his neck.

Never had blood tasted so sweet. She took her fill and then some, draining every last drop from the handler, siphoning what remained even after the poor bastard's heart had stopped. This man represented everything she'd held in for thirty years, all of her aggression and all of her past grievances, and when she dropped his lifeless, used up body on the ground, a weight lifted from her shoulders.

There would be more, sure, but this one sated something deep within her that went beyond simple bloodlust.

Satisfied for the moment, Mira's senses were sharp, aided by the fresh blood flowing through her. Below her, the Magistrate was not unconscious like he was pretending to be. The pattern of his breath was too anxious. Rapid uneven breaths; yet his eyes remained closed. Crafty bastard, what is he playing at now? Mira wondered.

Hairs on the back of her neck tingled. She felt the break of air near her, but before anything could strike, a male groaned behind her. She turned, meeting the brilliant fangs of Stryker as he held a handler one-armed up in the air. In his other hand was a UV torch.

"How do you like them?" Stryker asked before bludgeoning the handler with his own weapon. Stryker's first hit dented the human's skull with a sickening thud, and he was dead before the second hit landed.

"I could have taken him," Mira said, watching Stryker toss the lifeless body to the ground.

"Just say thank you."

She met his eyes, wondering what he meant by that. She could have taken the human easily enough. She'd have thanked him on her own, but hearing him practically demand it of her rubbed her the wrong way.

There was a smile behind those amber eyes, though, that helped disarm her. Mira felt a snarky smile of her own raising the corners of her mouth.

"Even warriors need someone to watch their backs." Stryker's tone softened.

"Yeah, right… thanks," Mira said, and turned back toward the Magistrate, only to find that he'd managed to roll away and disappear into the crowd while her back had been turned. "Shit! He's gone."

"I'm on it." Stryker dove into the crowd of brawling people.

Mira scanned from her position, hoping to catch a tiny glimpse of him, cursing herself for letting Stryker distract her from her duty. Another thought suddenly struck her. Where was Lucian? Surrounding her was a mass of bloody, writhing, fighting bodies. Even with her own enhanced senses, Mira had a hard time deciphering who was who. The only thing she could tell for sure was that handlers were wearing black.

"Mira."

She heard her name being called out over the fray. Scanning the crowd again, she tried to spot the man searching for her.

"Mira!" The voice took on a frantic tone.

There, to her left. She saw Lucian. And behind him, the Magistrate had the blade of a short sword – her sword – at his neck.

Where and how he'd managed to grab it was a secondary thought. Getting to him before the Magistrate slit his throat was most important, and that was going to be tricky.

Stryker had spotted him too, but just like a wolf, he was lying in wait for the right time to strike.

Mira met the Magistrate's eyes, daring him to make a move.

The Magistrate, sword at Lucian's throat, slowly backed away from the fighting hoard.

Using her eyes, Mira tried to communicate with Stryker, telling him to follow close but not to attack. She wasn't sure he'd gotten the actual message, but Stryker slowly prowled through the fight towards the Magistrate.

More aware of her surroundings than she must have looked, Mira quickly side-stepped a blow from behind. Another handler, foolish enough to try her, met a quick end. Not wanting to waste any time or energy, she snapped his neck and dropped him to the ground.

The Magistrate was getting close to an alleyway nearby. He'd cleared the fight and still had Lucian by the neck. She stalked into the crowd after them, making quick work of any human that came across her path.

"You'll never make it out alive if you harm him," Mira warned, as she found the mouth of the alleyway. "Drop the weapon and let Lucian go. Don't be a fool. You know I have you outnumbered here. Your handlers are all dead or dying now. How long do you think you'll survive out there, on your own?"

He hesitated. It was merely a heartbeat, but that was long enough for Mira to strike. Using all the speed she could muster, she was on the bloated human before he could contemplate making a move. She gripped the hilt of the sword and simultaneously pulled it away and pushed Lucian down. With a spin, she disarmed the Magistrate and brought the hilt of the weapon down on his head, knocking him out for sure this time. "Stupid human." She spat at his unconscious body, lying like a blob of putrid flesh on the ground.

"Hey!" Lucian's enraged tone failed to garner the response he must have wanted, and when he put a hand on Mira, she almost took it off.

"Don't leave my side again if you want to live. You hear me?"

"I don't…"

"Your value at the moment is in information and directions. Don't wander off in this mass of shit." She waved behind her at the simmering battle still claiming its last few victims. "You can't fight. You're not Immortal. You're as good as dead." Mira hadn't truly meant to insult, but her stress levels had reached a height she could hardly fathom. It was one thing for her to worry for her own life, but protecting others… that was a whole new game. One she was being forced to play.

"Sorry."

Smart man, Mira thought. She picked up the fallen sword and inspected it. Her own blade. The same one she had always chosen in the stables. The familiar weight of it brought her comfort, but she couldn't understand why. That weapon had been one of her bondage. For that reason alone it should have made her cringe, but like an old friend, it brought warmth and lessened her stress level.

"What now?" Stryker asked.

"Bring the Magistrate. We still need him."

Stryker nodded and lifted the unconscious man.

The battle dying down, it was truly time for them to get out of the city. Mira rounded up the vampires, and they commandeered as many transports as they could find. Though for the moment they were victorious, Mira felt as if they had probably made things worse. Only time would tell, though, and they were running out of it. Sunrise would come soon, and they still had to make it to a safe place.

CHAPTER TWELVE

J**ust as the sky was beginning** to lighten, they rendezvoused with the rest of the Otherkin in a surprisingly close location. Mira had assumed they'd all be traveling back to Caldera to deal with the Magistrate, but when Jay, their messenger bird met them at the city gates, she led them only a few miles west.

A small city of tents lay before them in a small valley with a river. Mira had not thought it possible, but by all appearances, the Otherkin had amassed an army, and in only a few days' time. Clearly the Otherkin Council was preparing for war. She wondered if they had pulled every able body from the city.

Mira remained skeptical, though. These Otherkin might have numbers and shiny new weapons, but their people were not battle-ready. Her crew were tough warriors – vampire gladiators, all of them. She hoped they'd still be willing to take up the cause now that they had fulfilled their first agreement to her. But if they did not, these Otherkin would be massacred.

The Council knew they were coming; most had assembled in front of the tent city to welcome them. They pulled their transports up in front of the largest tent, and Mira and Stryker exited first, holding the Magistrate as a gift to the awaiting council members.

Against the odds, Alec looked pleased to see them, though his smile did not much improve the look of his face.

"The vampires are free," Mira proclaimed. "And the city is leaderless."

Stryker set down the Magistrate at Alec's feet and kicked him just enough to wake him. The Magistrate grumbled and groaned, then reality lit his eyes with fear.

"What... where have you taken me?" He scrambled to get up, tripping over his purple robes and sending dust flying up in the air.

"Silence," Mira commanded. "You will speak when spoken to."

Pure waves of hatred flowed from Magistrate's eyes, but he held his tongue and sat on the ground at her feet.

Alec's smile turned wicked. "This offering pleases us."

Not sure what exactly he meant by that, Mira had no immediate response.

Michael came out of the large tent to greet Mira. "The warrior returns victorious." All congeniality aside, she could see the astonishment in his eyes. Perhaps he hadn't expected her to live, and even more shockingly, she'd returned with a living breathing Magistrate.

Troublesome as the Magistrate was, Mira was as good as her word. She'd brought him alive from the city to face judgment. The Magistrate's fate, however, would now rest with the very hungry-looking vampire Council member. "Well done. Well done." Michael eyed the overstuffed human cowering on the ground. "Bring him to us."

Mira grabbed the Magistrate's arm and hauled him up to his feet. "What is to happen now?"

"Our deal has been completed. You and your three human friends will be allowed permanent residency in Caldera Grove."

Mira cast a quick glance to Lucian who was exiting his transport vehicle. A sigh of relief escaped her involuntarily. He, as well as Curtis and Sarah, would be safe. She'd done all that had been requested of her. She'd jumped through so many hoops to get to this point. As much as she wanted to wash her hands of all the bloodshed and violence, she knew there was still so much more she had to do before sanctuary could well and truly be hers.

"What of my people?" Mira asked with a little apprehension. No one had agreed to anything beyond escaping the prison. They were free to do as they wished, and Mira knew that more than a few of them would rather not be under the thumb of a new leader.

"The vampires?" Michael waved a hand dismissively. "They are all our kind. They will be granted access to Sanctuary as well. Of course, that's assuming they are willing to join our cause."

She'd expected as much. Nothing was ever simple. "They have their own will. I cannot speak for them all, but" – she turned back and met Tegan's anticipatory glare – "I have a feeling the prospect of more bloodshed would sit well with most."

"War is bloody." Michael smiled, and his fangs glistened in the waning moonlight. "I'm sure your friends will want to savor the spoils."

More fighting. Mira was sick of the constant battle. She hadn't stopped fighting since the day she'd been tossed into the arena. When will it all be over?

"Before anyone agrees to any new fights, we need our rest." Mira nodded to the sky growing ever lighter above them.

"Of course. We have a tent waiting for you all. If you'll just hand him over…" Michael reached out and gripped the Magistrate's meaty arm.

At first, Mira hesitated, but she'd rather not have to babysit the murderous human all day; she needed her rest too. And the

Council was now in charge of his pathetic existence. She'd done her part.

"Take him." She let go of the Magistrate and wiped his sweat off her hands.

Though she was happy to be rid of him, the Magistrate suddenly looked like a frightened child. Being manhandled by a strange vampire, she almost felt sorry... almost. He wasn't worth her pity no matter how sad his puffy eyes got.

The sun was rising fast. Already in the gray light of early morning, Mira could feel the sting. "Time to find that tent," she urged.

Michael smiled, eyeing his prey hungrily, and led the way down a long row of tents. "We will all talk of what is to come after a well-deserved rest."

CHAPTER THIRTEEN

Despite a mind swarming with "what if's," Mira fell into a deep sleep, waking hours after the sun had set. When she finally made her way outside, she found the encampment alive with music and raucous voices. A few of her own vampire kin strolled by, laughing and patting each other on the back.

"What's going on?" she asked.

"Celebration time. The Council has thrown us a welcome party." The vampire sounded, if at all possible, drunk.

"And the refreshments…?"

"They have donors."

"Otherkin?"

"Yeah… but they take this special herb first and you feel…"

"Drunk." Mira shook her head. There was more to these Otherkin than she knew. But Lucian's remark about them being tricksters stuck in her mind.

"Just be careful."

"We're good." The vampire stumbled away, still chuckling with his friend.

Mira wandered through the tents, listening to the drunken conversations and atta boys going on all around. She was glad to see everyone getting on so well, but couldn't find that lightness of spirit yet herself.

"You should be celebrating." Stryker found her standing alone outside of the command tent. He strolled up casually, drink in hand. Mira caught a slight tang of alcohol on his breath. He must have been celebrating with the others.

She should have been celebrating. "I will. Just collecting my thoughts."

"You seem troubled."

"What exactly will happen to the Magistrate?"

"Getting soft on him, are you?"

"No. Nothing like that. Just… I want to be sure we're doing the right thing. We need peace. Not more aggression. Can we trust that the elders here will work towards peace, or…"

"Will they exact revenge?" Stryker asked.

"Yeah. Took the words right out of my mouth. I think they just want a bloody show and have no desire to end the aggression. What do you think?"

"Dunno. I'm not privy to all the decisions being made about our future, but I would like to think they'll do what's best for our people. They didn't earn their place as high elders by making poor decisions."

"Oh. I didn't mean to make it sound like that."

"I know."

"I just…"

"Don't trust anyone."

"Exactly."

"You're going to have to learn to," Stryker said and offered his hand. "Starting with me." He pulled her in close. Closer than she was comfortable with. The hardness of his body pressed tight against her own as his arms wrapped around her. It was a little too much to handle. She'd never been claustrophobic before, but even out in the open air, she was beginning to feel as if the walls were closing in on her. Stryker looked down, finding her eyes. "I like you, Mira, but you have to let your guard down."

His lips, so close she could feel the warmth of his breath washing down on her. How had she never stopped to admire them? And those sunny amber eyes, warm and inviting, practically begging to delve deep into her soul. He was more than a temptation. A perfect specimen of a man, but too much to handle at that moment.

Mira pushed against the hard wall of his chest. "I need air."

"Why?"

"You're too close."

"It's okay. No one's going to hurt you. Especially not me... You'd wipe the floor with me if I tried."

"True." She laughed, and some of the tension faded. "I'm just not used to people being so close, unless I'm about to kill them."

"I'm aware of that. But you have to learn to let down your guard. Let people get close. You're free now; you're safe."

"Free, yes. Safe, debatable. We're on the brink of war. No matter what's been said, we can't just walk away and go sit in the safety of Caldera. We're here. They're planning something. We have to stay and fight or whatever..."

"Yes, we'll probably be called into fight. But you don't have to fight me. That's what I'm saying." He closed in again, that hard body of his colliding with hers in a way that sent a shiver down her spine. Deep down, feelings stirred. Feelings she'd not let surface in far too long. She could see a future with him. Immortal, like her. Free, like her. Handsome, capable, strong, and a gentleman too. But with those feelings came anxiety. Letting someone in just led to more pain. The sharp sting of Theo's death had left a scar deep within her heart that she feared might never heal. She never wanted to feel that pain ever again. No, this had to stop.

"Let me in. Let me be close to you. Let us enjoy this night," he practically purred in her ear. The warmth of his voice was so tempting. The heat radiating off his body too delicious.

She wanted to be able to do all of that and more, but the anxiety was there, eating away at all of the pleasurable sensations. "Enough, Stryker."

Despite her warning, he refused to back down. His hand came up and caressed her cheek. "Tomorrow will come, and it will bring its problems, but tonight, we are free to enjoy ourselves."

She cringed at his touch, anxiety boiling over to the surface. This had to stop. In the space of a heartbeat she snatched his hand, spun him around, and pulled his wrist hard up behind his back. "I like you, but I said enough. Understand?"

"Don't break it... I might need that hand to fight later." With all the dignity of an alpha, he relaxed in her grip but did not verbally acknowledge defeat. Mira let him go, and when he turned back to meet her eyes, she saw admiration more than annoyance there. He held both hands up in surrender. "Another time, perhaps."

The sound of Lucian behind her clearing his throat startled Mira. Though there was no reason to, she suddenly felt shame for letting Stryker get so close. Why? Neither man had any claim to her, and yet, the feeling was there. She turned slowly, hoping to find his expression neutral, but there was pain behind his mossy eyes.

Stryker nodded at Lucian as he passed him, but neither man said a word. Awkward, but civil, thankfully.

"Have any news?" Mira kept her tone even, addressing the confused look on Lucian's face.

"No. Did you expect I would? Without you by my side, I'm a ghost to these people." Hurt was behind his words, but not for the snub of the Otherkin.

Why did men need to be so testy? Emotions were annoying things. Her own raw feelings were a testament to that. Best to bury them down deep where they couldn't be a bother.

Fighting her own awkward feelings, she tried to meet Lucian's eyes and pretend everything was normal. "They'll warm up to you eventually."

"Sure. Right after they're done slaughtering my people."

Mira shrugged. Her people had been slowly slaughtered for years. "We're at war. Be glad you're on the right side."

"I doubt either side has it right."

That piqued her curiosity. "What do you mean?"

"You value peace, as do I. We were both raised incorrectly. We both want for the best. But do you honestly think that the war the Council is trying to wage is the right approach?"

"No. Of course not, but that is what must come to pass to create change."

"Spoken like a warrior."

"You say that like it's a bad thing. It's what your people made me."

"And that is a bad thing. I know you're are more than just a warrior. I know deep down you have no taste for all this bloodshed and violence. All you've truly fought for since I met you has been peace." He might call it peace, but all she really desired was to stop having to fight. If that meant everyone was at peace, great.

"Even if you were right, there's nothing else I can do. I have no authority among these people. I'm a pawn in their game."

"And yet you've forced your hand with them already, securing a home for me, Curtis, and his wife."

Mira looked down, not deserving of such high praise. She kicked at the dirt with her sandal-clad foot. "I wouldn't call that deal a complete win for me. We're lucky to be alive after that suicide mission."

He reached out and placed a hand on her shoulder. "What I'm saying is this. You have more power than you think."

Mira had to fight the urge to jerk from his grip. Just as with Stryker touching her, Lucian's friendly gesture brought up feelings she did not have the capability of dealing with at the moment. Lucian must have recognized her discomfort; the hand vanished from her shoulder as he continued. "You know an all-out war is not going to bode well for either side. Speak your thoughts to the Council. Make them see reason, and maybe another option can be found."

There was truth behind his words. Mira wasn't a warmonger. She despised the thought of more fighting, but doubted she could get the Council to listen to her. She'd already overplayed her hand. But, as she looked up and met Lucian's hopeful eyes, she found strength. If nothing else, she could at least question the Council on their plans and maybe nudge them toward a solution that involved less bloodshed.

"Why do you have to be so damn good-natured? You're an Elite, for gods' sake."

Amused laughter brightened Lucian's face. "You say that like it's a bad thing."

"In my line of work, it is."

"I was privileged, yes, but not without schooling. Not all of my class used what they were taught, but that doesn't mean I am boorish. Just as you're not the savage you were trained to be."

"Such an unlikely pair." She hadn't meant to imply anything by it, but the light in Lucian's eyes said he took their unintention-al link personally.

"We do make quite the odd couple. Now, should I escort you to the Council's command tent?" He held his arm bent to escort her.

CHAPTER FOURTEEN

Two **Otherkin were standing guard** outside of the command tent. Mira sized them up as she approached with Lucian. Not particularly intimidating, they were both tall and thin, and looked like a good gust of wind would blow them over, but she wasn't going to let that fool her. Knowing now that they all possessed unique abilities put her on alert.

"Step aside; I am going inside," she commanded as she approached.

Her jaw almost hit the ground when they stood to the side and waved her to the open flap on the tent. "They've been waiting on you."

Mira wanted to throw a snippy comment their way, but she wasn't given the option. For once, they were doing exactly what she wanted. Something was wrong.

Eyeing them narrowly as she entered the tent, Mira wondered exactly was going on. Not as lavish as their conference room back in Caldera, the command tent looked quite comfy. All of the Council members sat on large cushions in a circle.

"…the dam is under our control." Alec was speaking, and seemed overly pleased with himself. "The shifters are on patrol, and we've shut down all water and power to the city."

"Well, that's one way to kick a hornets' nest." Mira spoke loudly enough to grab the attention of everyone in the room.

Alec, sitting closest to the entrance, turned his eyes on her. His lips stretched wide into a smile that made him look more troll than man. She wondered if trolls were part of the Otherkin, or just some pretend creature. "Mira... Just the vampire we were waiting on. When can your troops be ready to fight?"

She looked away, focusing on the canvas walls of the tent, remembering his handy little gift for meddling with people's minds. "You'll have to ask them. They are not my troops. They are free vampires."

"Who trust you and look up to you." Alec was really laying it on thick. His normal undertones of animosity were gone.

She had to suppress a laugh. "You're joking, right?"

"They owe you allegiance."

"They owe nothing to anybody. They've been paying for years. You want fighters, you ask them... nicely." She wasn't going to let him sweet talk her, and made damn sure to avoid eye contact with him to ensure there was no way he could meddle.

Michael stood and walked over to Mira. "We hoped you would act as a liaison. They know you. Come, join us here and let's discuss." He pointed to a vacant cushion on the ground near where he sat.

Mira wasn't in the 'sitting and chatting kum ba yah' mood. She needed to make her point and move on. Standing firm in her spot, she addressed the group. "Why must we fight? Surely there's a way to find peace without more bloodshed. Michael, was it not you who said that all you wanted was an end to the hostility between our two groups?"

Michael nodded. "Yes, but to end the hostility we must snip out the elements that are feeding the lies about our kind."

"Don't sugar coat. There is no 'snipping' here." Emotion colored her voice more than she had wanted it to. "You are planning war. You know who fights wars? The grunts. People who have no real opinion but who are told when and where to fight for their leaders. Are you going to stand next to your warriors and risk death on the battlefield?"

"We'll have no choice. By tomorrow they'll seek us out." Alec's smile turned truly wicked. For the first time she saw what could only be the demon inside of the man.

Eyes wide with fear of the unknown, Mira was almost afraid to ask. "What have you done?"

"We've forced their hand."

Roseanna, Alec's Otherkin partner, opened her mouth to speak, but before the words could escape her lips, Alec hushed her with a look. Mira had noticed on quite a few occasions that the female had been all but mute in their gatherings; something she would have to focus on later. Alec's revelation had a lump of fear forming in her chest.

"How exactly have you forced their hand?" she asked tentatively.

"Without power and water, humans cannot live. They'll either flee their city or meet us head on to reclaim what they've lost. And we will be ready either way to take the city."

Mira tried to force down the lump. They had riled up the humans, that was for sure. But had they considered the fallout? "You'll not have your vampire warriors if they decided to fight you during the day."

"Vampires can fight inside." Alec pointed down to a map lying on the ground in the center of their circle. Next to that was a set of blueprints. Niko and Katerina were both busily poring over the layout, talking amongst themselves. They glanced up and nodded at Mira, and then immediately went back to the blue-prints.

"As you have probably guessed, our shifters are plotting the best defense of the outside, while you and your kind will guard the inside. If the humans should meet us during daylight, they will still be defeated. "

Fighting indoors, in an enclosed environment. That was just asking for trouble; but if the sun was out, there was nothing else to do. What a terrible plan.

"And what of the Magistrate?" she asked, wondering what more terrible ideas they had in store.

Now it was Natasha's turn to respond. "Don't concern your-self with him. He'll be given the same treatment that he gave to our kind. Justice will be dealt." Fangs glistening with hunger, she looked more than eager to dole out that punishment.

"You mean revenge." If anyone was going to exact revenge, it really should have been Mira and her vampire brethren. They had been the ones to suffer at his hands. But that was an argument for a different day.

"Call it what you will."

"We'll come back to that. His punishment should really be something public, and not just for the sake of my brothers in arms, but for the humans too."

"You do what you do best – fight. Let the Council handle the important matters."

It was all she could do to bite her tongue and not his head off for a comment like that. Of all the Otherkin, Alec rubbed her the wrong way most of all. She sensed the hatred was equal between them both. Unlikely allies for the present; but for how long, she wondered?

The Magistrate issue would have to be dealt with later, and she made a mental note to come back to it if they survived the next battle, but the war that was about to begin had to take precedence. "I will fight. Not for you, though," she sneered at Alec, but made sure not to maintain eye contact. "And my kin will fight too... because you have forced their hand. They will do it for survival. I did not free them so they could be slaves to different masters."

Natasha held up a perfectly manicured finger. "Ah, but Mira, they are fighting for their freedom. That is far from being forced to kill each other in the arena."

"Only someone who has never been there would say that." She doubted the pampered vampire had ever fought more than a bad hair day in her immortal life.

Sirens went off outside. A moment later, a loud blast shook the tent they were standing in.

"Well, you were right about one thing: they came looking," Mira muttered, and turned for the exit.

Outside, sirens blared. The enemy was close. Scurrying people darted in and out of the camp, some frantically grasping at weapons and others looking as if they were hoping for a safe place to hide. An uneasy feeling tiptoed up Mira's spine, settling at the base of her neck with a nagging ache. She took a deep breath. No matter what she wanted, peace was always one more battle away.

There was no time for moral objections. Mira sprinted down towards the tents her comrades had been assigned.

"Find a weapon, boys. Time for a fight," she said, entering the tent with as much arrogant importance as she could muster.

"I'm assuming the sirens mean we have company." George's tone failed to hide the anguish behind his eyes.

"We're not done fighting for our freedom. One last battle awaits." Mira hated having to say the words. Lies, all lies. She knew she'd just traded in one master for another. But, in order to survive to fight the political battle another day, she had to muster her people to fight the physical battle this night.

Expecting to hear the groans and complaints from the weary warriors, she was shocked when one by one, those who were in the tent rose, ready to fight.

Her chest swelled with pride. Though no one said it, they respected her and would follow her into battle without question. She was their leader.

More vampires poured into the tent as the sirens continued, looking for answers and instructions. Mira gave the same speech to them.

All except Tegan. He scoffed at her request to take up arms. "I didn't sign up for any of this."

"None of us did. We've all been screwed. Is that what you wanted to hear?"

"At least you admit it."

"Much good it does. We still have to fight if we want to have our freedom."

"Always one more fight…"

"Yeah. And whining about it like a baby doesn't change that fact. Find whatever motivation you need – revenge, whatever – and get out there and defend this camp."

A loud boom shook the ground, followed by painful cries. It was enough to snap both warriors to attention. Tegan picked up his weapon. "This isn't over between us. I'm not your pawn, you hear me?"

"Never said you were. Fight me later. But now, we have a job to do. Get out there and fight as if your life depends on it… Because it just might. I'll be right behind you." She'd join the fight soon enough, but needed to find her humans first.

"Not good enough." Tegan snatched her hand as she was leaving the tent. "You fight with us."

"Release me. I'll be there in a moment. I just need to check…"

"If you want these men to follow you to the grave, then show them what kind of leader you are."

"Last warning. Release my arm before I pull yours from the socket and beat you bloody with it."

"Let her go, man. We have a fight at our door." George stood tall and closed in.

"I just want the human-lover to show us who is most important to her. I know she's running off to check on that Elite."

Mira snarled and threw her arm back, twisting out of Tegan's grip. Before he could react, she pulled his arm up behind his back. "You know what's important to me? Peace. I'm sick of fighting: you, humans, everyone! You want to be a petty little crybaby about this, then leave. No one wants you here. Otherwise, get out there and help us win this stupid war. I'll be right there behind you all."

Tegan grunted. Mira took that as his acquiescence and released him. She turned to George. "I promise, I'll be right behind you. I just need to make sure Lucian is safe."

"I understand. Go." George, always level-headed; she knew he truly did understand.

Mira bolted out of the tent, but not before she heard Tegan's grumble of "Human-lover" under his breath.

She made a mental note to make him pay for that comment later.

Though Lucian had been close behind her when she went to the command tent, she had not seen him since she'd gone inside.

There had to be at least a hundred tents in their encampment. He could be anywhere, even out fighting. Assuming, though, that he'd not gone too far, Mira headed back toward the command tent. Like the rush of flooding waters, everyone in the camp was heading out to meet the battle head on, but she fought the current.

Behind the command tent, two Otherkin stood guard over a smaller tent. Everyone else in the camp was rushing away; why weren't they?

Intuition told her that she'd find him there, so she walked straight up to the taller of the two guards. "I need to go inside."

"No, you don't." The male was confident, and he met Mira's eyes with no sign of apprehension.

She wasn't falling for that again.

"Your tricks don't work on me, but mine will certainly work on you." Mira cracked her knuckles and simultaneously licked her fangs.

A silent battle was being fought behind the Otherkin's eyes. He quickly glanced to his partner, as if looking for help.

"Do you know how many I've fought and killed bare-handed in the arenas? I don't want to, but if you don't let me, I will kill you to get inside that tent."

The soldier's shoulders slumped. "We were given orders…" She could tell he didn't want to fight but couldn't disobey his masters either. She wondered if their mental tricks went as far as complete compulsion.

"I'm sorry," she said with a sigh, and then threw a lightning-quick right cross, connecting with the guard's jaw."

His head snapped to the side and he dropped without so much as a groan. He'd be down for the count for a while, but she could still hear his heartbeat. He'd survive this.

Blinding light flashed in her face. She'd hardly heard the click of the UV torch being turned on, nor expected such a thing from her own kind. Hissing in pain, she swatted blindly at the light. "What the hell?"

"You are not authorized," he said with far less conviction than someone in his position should have.

The light seared her skin and burned her eyes. No matter how many times she'd been punished with this in the past, she still had not developed an immunity to its sting. Hurt brought rage. Rage made her even more deadly. Squeezing her eyes shut against the pain, she tried to lunge forward, but before she could get far, something hard and heavy came down on the back of her head.

She dropped to the ground and instinctively rolled to the side to avoid another hit from whatever it was that had clubbed her. Ears ringing and a massive headache developing did not improve her mood. She hadn't wanted to kill the guards before, but now this one was just asking for it. She'd enjoy his healing blood when this fight was over.

"Come no closer, vampire. You are not authorized."

"You, sir, are a dead man," Mira promised, pain urging her on.

She moved with lightning speed, diving at his ankles and knocking him off balance before he could aim another hit at her. The UV torch fell from his grasp and rolled away. He scrambled to get it, but she was already on him. Not even giving him a chance to say his last words, she dove at his neck. Hot, fresh blood soothed the aches and pains of her fresh wounds. Her ears stopped ringing almost immediately, but the headache would take a little longer to subside. Though she'd promised death, she left the soldier alive, though too weak to move. They all might want to paint her as a killer, but she was far from it.

Lucian sat just inside the tent, tied to a chair, next to the Magistrate. She'd expected as much for that pompous overfed Elite, but not for Lucian. He'd been promised sanctuary! She wondered about the fate of Curtis and Sarah. She hadn't seen them since they'd parted ways in Caldera.

Before she could step further into the tent, another blast of searing light stole her vision.

"I had a feeling I'd see you in here sooner or later." She couldn't see him, but she knew the voice. Alec.

"You made a promise." Mira's rasped, pain stealing her voice.

"Yes, I did give my blood oath. But the thing is, you're not a resident of Caldera. You are not one of my people, so… I'm afraid the promise is actually worthless."

Her eyes twitched, struggling to stay open and still avoid the bright light.

"You see, I need assurances that you and your people will fight."

"What do you think we're doing, you bastard?"

"But you are here… go out now and fight. No harm will come to your human if you do."

Every word out of his mouth was a lie. There was no way she was leaving her friend here with him now. "No harm will come to him no matter what I do."

"That's not entirely true. I have a blade at his throat right now. If you turn around and leave, I'll not use it to slice open his throat. However, if you so much as take a step in the wrong direction, I will not hesitate to end him."

"Then you'll have broken your blood oath."

"And I'll have to kill you as well, so no one will know of my transgression."

"Empty threat."

"You think I can't kill you?"

"Oh, I'm quite sure you can't. But I'd love to see you try. Put down the weapons and let's fight as nature intended, hand to hand and fang to… Well, whatever you have."

Alec chuckled. "You assume I would fight fair. How sweet."

Her first instinct was to use all of her supernatural speed and hope she could get to Alec before he sliced through Lucian's throat, but doubt held her back. He'd anticipate something like that for sure.

It took all the strength she had inside to keep herself calm as she addressed the Otherkin leader. "Kill him, then."

"What did you say?" The shock in his voice amused her. She only wished she could see the look on his face. If not for that damn light...

"Do it. He's your guarantee that I'll get my vampires to perform... so kill him. We're done fighting other's battles. And then I can have the pleasure of killing you."

Alec lowered the UV torch, allowing Mira to see his hand clutching the knife at Lucian's throat. "I think you're bluffing. I know how much this one means to you. You'll do anything to ensure his survival."

"He's human... for him, death is inevitable."

"You love him. You'd turn him eventually."

Love? Did she love him? That was such a foreign word to her. She cared for him. She could not imagine him not being part of her life, but was that love? Maybe. Again with those messy feelings. She didn't have time for them to cloud her thoughts. "I'm not going to debate with you. Kill him or don't, that's your choice. I will not be commanded by the likes of you or anyone else anymore."

He hesitated for the briefest of seconds, but it was enough for Mira to spring into action. She was on Alec before he could take the deadly swipe with his blade. Grabbing him at the wrists, she snapped his arm back, crushing it in her hand. With the grace of a dancer, she spun the little man around, still keeping his knife hand in check, and drew it right up to his own carotid artery. "I never trusted you for one second." She bent down close to his ear. "For the record… my people were already out fighting your war. You'd have known that if you were in the battle too, instead of cowering behind others." She slit his throat cleanly and dropped the blade to the ground.

The once-proud Otherkin leader gurgled and groaned as the life drained from his body. All the while those hate-filled eyes stared up at her, condemning her for her actions, until the light finally left them.

When his body went still, she left him on the floor and used the knife to cut the ties around Lucian's arms and legs.

"You didn't have to do that," Lucian said.

"Actually, I did. He would have never let there be peace. The others, maybe; but this one never showed any sympathy for outsiders… even my kind."

"Thank you."

She turned on him, rage coloring her words, angry for all the blood on her hands. "Don't ever thank me for killing someone."

CHAPTER FIFTEEN

From one fight to the next, Mira rejoined her brothers in arms on the battlefield, a seemingly endless stream of displaced hanger and hatred ending only with the swing of her sword.

The battle raged all night. Not a single soul had escaped the fight. Signs of it were everywhere. Mira looked down at her hands. Blood and gore coated her sword, and her fingernails caked with dirt and grime. It was the arena all over again, just on a larger scale. Faces of all the humans she'd had to destroy added to the others already haunting her dreams.

"When will it end?" she screamed

As the sun began to lift over the horizon, Mira saw more than just her own horror: the utter devastation that is war.

The Otherkin were claiming it as a victory, but how could anyone celebrate such utterly pointless slaughter?

"Regroup," she called out to her people. The sun's early rays were already stinging her eyes. She waved them on and headed back to the camp and the safety of their tent.

Alec's blood stained the ground, bleeding out of the tent where she'd left him. Mira's nostrils flared as she walked past, inhaling the intensity of his scent. She'd intended to take refuge in her own tent, but she bumped into Michael on the way.

"Who did this?" Michael eyes went wide as saucers as he took in the sight of all the blood caking the ground.

"I did." Mira didn't hesitate to answer, looking Michael straight in his eyes.

He moved in a flash and had her by the throat. "Give me one reason…"

She stared directly into his angry eyes. "He gave a blood oath. He lied. I made him pay."

"You have proof of this? Or just your word?"

"I have nothing to prove to you or anyone else here," she hissed. "Drop me now before I make you pay the same debt your friend did."

She couldn't see them, but she knew other vampires – her kin – were closing in, surrounding Michael and her.

He dropped her and grumbled under his breath, "Casualty of war." His eyes darted every which way, stopping for moments on each face around him before moving to the next. She wasn't sure if it was their presence that had stopped him from a futile attempt to punish her, or the fact that he had an oath to honor as well.

"We've fought your war. We've done everything asked of us. As of now, I release my people from any service to the Otherkin." Mira was done as well, although she knew the war wasn't truly over.

The rage in Michael's eyes subsided. "We need to take shelter now from the sun. Please, step inside." He ushered her as well as the vampires who'd come to her aid inside the command tent.

Somehow now, with only Michael there to represent the Council, the place felt less formal. The cushions had been piled in the center of the room, and Mira took one and collapsed on it, thankful to be off her feet.

"I guess we're stuck here for the day. That gives you plenty of time to talk." She directed her comment right at Michael.

Wearily, the others filtered in to the room and carved out spaces where they could sit. The whole lot of them were dirty and coated in a fine layer of blood. George in particular looked positively monstrous, his bald head sporting a huge gash that had scabbed over. It was healing, but he looked terrible with it. The entire group of vampires looked like the savages they'd been accused of being all those years in prison. And for the first time, Mira felt the title was right.

"What happened last night was a travesty. Needless deaths." She didn't know how many humans and Otherkin had died; the number really wasn't important, the fact that it should have been avoided was.

"What happened last night was necessary to break the humans' forces. We had to clear away the cancer, so that now we can go in and repair the damage."

"There is no repair for slaughter."

"You and I see things differently. I can appreciate that. Yours is the viewpoint from the sword. One I hope you will not have to use again." His words sounded nice, but she knew better than to believe them.

"You have done all that has been asked of you." Michael addressed the weary warriors like a proud general. It was then that Mira noticed that, unlike anyone in her group, Michael was clean; he hardly had a speck of dirt on him. "Today we rest, tomorrow we take the city."

How dare he act as if he were one of them, fighting with them, patting them on the back for helping his cause, when he hadn't had the balls to face the battle himself? She gritted her teeth, hundreds of nasty thoughts and words swarming around her brain.

"You warriors have earned a place of honor in our city. When you return with us to Caldera, you will be treated as heroes."

She wanted to say the harsh things she felt at that moment, but her brothers in arms needed this kudos. They'd fought hard for a cause that was not their own. Granted, most of them were taking revenge, but they shouldn't have had to fight in the first place.

Michael continued his platitudes. "You, though, Mira, I honor most of all. You shall be made a general. And with that, I ask to stay at our side and lead your people as we take the city tomorrow."

"Why?" Her eyes narrowed suspiciously on Michael. "We were supposed to be free to go to live in peace. Why are you changing the deal now?"

Michael knelt down before Mira. "You're a figurehead. The people know you. Know of your strength and cunning. To see you lead former slaves back into the city will send a strong message. We'll use that to avoid further altercations during our occupation of the city."

It was never-ending. She'd never be free. Never see the end of the fighting. Never be her own person. Slave to the humans or slave to the Otherkin, she could never be her own master. "And if I refuse?"

"You won't." Michael stood and paced the room, arms crossed behind his back, looking at the other vampires as he passed them. "You know as well as I that your presence among these people will work towards non-violent resolutions to our differences. They will be too afraid to rise up with you and the rest of your warriors there as enforcers."

No use complaining about it; she'd just have to make the best of her situation. If the Otherkin wanted to play games with her, she'd play them right back. "Then I demand a place among the Council. I hear you have an opening."

"Cute," Michael's tone said anything but that. "I cannot, however, offer that position to you. You do not speak for any sect of people."

"I speak for my people. Those vampires of the Iron Gate." Mira stood and waved a hand towards her comrades. "These are not your pathetic and weak city-dwellers. These are hardened warriors who do not pander to leaders they could crush under their sandals."

That got Michael's attention. Anger flashed in his eyes, but he did not let his face betray the emotion.

"Think I'm wrong? Try me. Try any of my people." She side-stepped, giving Michael a full view of the vampires behind her. "Go ahead and try to take on any one of us. That's how a warrior earns their place in the pecking order. Or allow me to take a spot on the Council and represent them."

The heat of Michael's gaze could be felt by all, but he remained silent, seething while he again looked at the surrounding group of vampires. He might have the strength of a vampire, but he was not battle-worn like she and her kind were. Of that she was certain, and she was ready to test it if he didn't give in to her demands.

"You agree to accompany me into the city?"

"I will. But I will not force my people to do so."

Michael's eyes flitted to each vampire in the room before returning to Mira. "I will propose and offer my backing to elect you a member of the Council."

He'd given in faster than she'd expected, but that was still no guarantee.

Mira turned her back on Michael to address her people. "I will not ask any more from you all. You've served well and earned more than a rest. You all are free to leave. Make a home for yourselves in Caldera Grove."

George stood from his spot in the corner of the tent. "I'd follow you into the jaws of hell if you asked. I'll join your campaign back into the city."

"But I didn't ask—"

"You didn't have to. I'm not letting you go back into that city alone."

A true friend and ally. The thought of George by her side warmed her heart. "Thank you."

A few other vampires stepped forward as well, willing to act as a sort of entourage for her.

Surprisingly, Tegan too stepped forward. "I'm not saying I'll be your lackey or anything like that, but if I get the chance to put a few more humans in their place, I'm all for it."

Mira turned back to Michael, feeling more confident in her position. "I will return to the city with my crew. As long as I have your blood oath that you'll help install me on the Council."

"I'll do what I can, but no promises..."

"You'll do exactly what you promise, or I'll have your blood, just as I did Alec's."

She could see it in Michael's eyes and the way he chewed his tongue. Men hated to be backed into a corner with no way out, and it was obvious he desperately wanted to squash her like a bug. She knew she was probably overplaying her hand, but there was no other way around it. These Otherkin were not as trustworthy as she'd originally thought. Sanctuary, as perfect as it seemed, was not a true paradise, and if she wanted even some semblance of peace after all was said and done, she had to be in a position to push for it herself.

She narrowed her eyes at him. He'd waited too long to respond. "Do we have a deal?"

"Fine. You have my … blood oath."

"We don't have to be enemies, you and I… remember that." Mira held her hand out to shake.

"We are not enemies." Michael took her outstretched hand in his and gave a quick pump before pulling back quickly.

She felt more his enemy now than she had been before. At least she had her people's support. She didn't know when it would happen, but she knew she'd already made it onto Michael's hit list.

CHAPTER SIXTEEN

F illed with victorious energy, the Otherkin army proudly marched through the Iron Gate of New Haven. Niko and Katerina took the lead, dragging the Magistrate, chained and gagged, through the city streets.

Behind them Mira, Stryker, and Lucian walked.

They in turn were followed by a mix of vampires, Otherkin, and Shifters, with the remainder of the Council. All together they were a formidable conquering army that anyone would be afraid to challenge.

Humans looked on from their homes, behind curtained windows, afraid to come out and see their new leaders. Mira could see the tiny faces of scared children peeking out though the windows. She remembered back to her first fight, seeing children sitting in the arena, watching and waiting for the battle to begin. Watching another's death had held no meaning then; but now, she could see the worry in their not-so innocent eyes.

Her resolve waivered. Peace. Could it really be? These children had been brought up on the blood sport and lies told by their parents. Their parents had left to fight a war and never returned. Retribution would be what sustained them, not compassion. They'd grow up to be the next group of haters and warmongers.

"You all right?" George's hand came down on her shoulder. She almost jumped at the unfamiliar touch.

"Careful, killer." He laughed nervously. "I've seen that look on you before. Those forlorn eyes."

"I'm good. Just a fleeting thought," Mira lied. The deeper they walked into the city, the more foreboding her thoughts became. They were an invading army. And this was only one city. There were many more human strongholds out there.

"You've always been a terrible liar. Just speak your mind." George knew her best. There was no point hiding anything from him.

"You know my mind. I don't want to be here. I don't think we should be here. Any of us. Peace will not come from occupying the human city, nor from the inevitable retribution from both sides." Mira looked out again at the buildings as they passed. It was like a ghost town, only she knew the inhabitants were still there, alive and scared.

"Have some faith. Things look ominous, but I'll be willing to bet these Otherkin and humans will surprise us."

"People of New Haven." Niko's voice boomed through the near silent streets. "The human reign of terror is over. We, the Otherkin, have control. This is our city now!"

Mira's shoulders slumped. Hundreds of years of life and experience, and that was the best Niko could say to the war-torn city dwellers? She turned a wary eye on George. "Surprised yet?"

George smiled weakly and shrugged.

Niko continued addressing the empty street. "Your presence is requested this evening in the arena where you have watched thousands of my brethren slaughter each other."

Mira nudged Niko. "Maybe we should try to kill them with kindness, rather than actually..."

"Any human who does not attend will be rounded up and brought to the arena by force."

"Never mind."

The Shifter leader regarded Mira sternly. "Thank you for your service, but now it is time to get to the business of running this city as our own. We need to make it quite clear to the humans who they belong to."

That was the last thing Mira wanted to hear. The cycle was starting again. Masters and slaves – only the positions had been changed. "No one belongs to anyone; that was the point of this." She tried to keep her tone even, but the more she had to endure, the harder it became. Images flashed before her of a time in the not-too-distant future where another rebellion would happen, and again, and again. Never-ending battles for supremacy.

"Don't be so literal," Niko scoffed.

A snippy reply was on the tip of her tongue, but before she could utter a word, Stryker grasped hold of her arm. Instinct more than anything else had her pivoting, trying to escape his grip while her other hand cocked back for a punch.

"Mira, wait." Stryker released her arm. "For the moment, we must remain unified. Let's settle this in closed quarters."

She met his eyes with rage at first, but those amber eyes were soft and filled with compassion, unlike the others. She lowered her arm. "You're right."

"Wait... did you just listen to me?" He smiled playfully, and didn't dodge when she smacked his shoulder.

Niko made his announcement again as they turned the corner and the arena in all its terrible glory came into view. Jutting up from the ground, a proud testament to human architecture, it was the largest building in the city.

She'd seen it so many times from the inside, but to see the exterior of the massive building with its domed roof in the light of the moon was devastatingly captivating. Memories flashed before her eyes. Countless deaths had come from that foul place. Cold dead stares, milky-white eyes, former friends and allies, all gone. And too many of them killed by her own hands.

She wasn't the only one feeling the building rage. Though he'd never admit to it, she could see it behind George's eyes. And others, still more vampires, upon seeing that building were overcome with emotion. Anger, rage, hatred… all because of the humans.

"Do I have to go in there?" Mira tried to keep her voice calm.

"Yes," Stryker answered. "But we'll be with you, and no one has to fight."

"That's not entirely true," Niko responded. "No one will be forced to fight… But I'm sure I'll have volunteers lined up."

Mira almost stopped dead in her tracks. If not for the hundreds behind her marching onward in the morbid parade, she would have. Fighting in the arena? That was how the Otherkin leaders were going to start their occupation of the city? That was how they planned on easing the humans into being okay under Otherkin rule?

No. This was not how it was supposed to be!

As they marched on toward the arena, Mira could hear the screams and cries of people being dragged from their houses, further confirming what she had already assumed. This was only the beginning, and fighting would continue. But, though she wanted to lash out, she knew Stryker was right – it was best to wait until they were out of the public view to settle things. She looked left to George and right where Lucian was standing. Behind her, Stryker was there too. Her three closest allies. Having them close gave her confidence that she could make a difference.

CHAPTER SEVENTEEN

The arena was packed, but instead of the sounds of cheering and drunken masses, there was silence. Eerie and disturbing, it was as if Death himself had taken up residence. Mira looked on from the Elite box where the rest of the Otherkin Council had set themselves up to view their games.

Stripped of her allies, Mira had to deal with the Council alone. Though it was slightly unnerving, Mira was certain she could either make them see reason or force her hand, if need be. What was one more death at that point? "End this madness," she sighed, watching a human dragged out to the center of the arena below.

"We must show them who is in charge here," Niko said, settling into a cushiony chair, looking out at the arena through the large glass window, ready to watch the carnage.

"By doing to them what they did to my people?" Mira asked indignantly. "Eye for an eye, eh?"

"It's what they understand." Natasha stood at the window, eagerly looking down at the humans seated below her. "We're only showing them the same courtesy they gave our kind."

"All you're doing is proving that we are no better than the savages they believed us to be." Mira hoped her calm approach would work. She already knew from a lifetime of personal experience that brute force wasn't the answer.

"We're doing them a service, showing them in this manner. We could just round the lot of them up and feed them to the troops. No humans, no more problem." Her words were as sharp as her fangs. Natasha glared at Mira in a way that a wolf would have taken as a challenge. But they were not pack animals, they were vampires. There was more to that stare than simple dominance. And Mira retuned it in kind.

"Peace was never in your game plan, was it?" It was all becoming painfully clear now.

"Peace comes in the end... when we have finished with the humans."

"You were human once..."

"I'm not anymore. I am better than them."

That was the final straw. She clenched her fist tight, sizing up the Council members in the room, mentally figuring out who best to take down first.

The door opened, startling her from her thoughts. She turned and came face to face with Tegan. Behind him, Otherkin soldiers entered brandishing swords. Mira knew from the moment Tegan stepped up to her that thing were going to get complicated.

"Let's make this easy, Mira," Tegan said hesitantly.

She'd fought the hulking vampire before. She knew she could take him, but there were too many others in the room. Out of the corner of her eye she caught the glint of light on metal, then came the click. Blinding light hit her square in the face. She wasn't sure what hurt worse – the sting of the light, or the betrayal of her own people, using the weapons of their captors on vampire kind!

She ducked low and swept Tegan's feet, hoping to knock him to the ground and maybe use his massive form as a shield, but before she could, others dove on top of her. Squirming as best she could, Mira wasn't able to stop them from pinning her arms and legs. Shrieking like a banshee, she fought hard to move her limbs, but it was no use. There were too many on her, and that damned light was blocking her vision.

"Let's take her to the prison and put her in her old cell." Mira didn't see Tegan's face, but it was he who uttered the words.

It took four soldiers and Tegan to get her downstairs and into the prison level. She fought and squirmed and cursed the whole way. But as soon as she saw what awaited her, Mira's voice fell silent.

George and Stryker were bent over a limp Lucian lying on the floor. Blood was in the air, and she knew exactly whom it belonged too.

Tegan pressed a few buttons on the keypad to her cell. She listened to the pattern, remembering the sounds she'd heard so many times.

Once the door was open, Tegan threw Mira hard onto the concrete floor in the cell. She almost trampled the others as she came crashing down.

"How could you turn your back on your people?" Mira shrieked after Tegan.

He turned around and faced her. "You betrayed us by being a human-lover. How many years have we been forced into killing our own kind? How much blood is on your hands? It's time for payback. Time to show the humans why we're the top of the food chain."

"What then? Killing, killing, and more killing? When does it end?"

"When the humans are dead."

"We were human once, Tegan."

"Well, we aren't anymore."

"Exactly. People can change."

"Spare me."

"Spare them. Teach them rather than kill them. Nothing good will come from mass extermination in the name of revenge."

"When did you become a peacekeeper?"

"I'm sick of killing, Tegan. Peace means no more killing. That's all I want, an end to violence. I've had my fill, and so have you. Look deep inside. Do you really want to continue blindly killing for whatever master you serve?"

"I serve no one!"

"Really? Then why are you at the Council's beck and call?"

"Our desires are aligned at the moment."

"And when they're not, what then? You'll end up in a cell just like me, just like when the humans turned on our kind years ago."

"Stop it. I don't need to listen to any of your nonsense. I have a fight coming up." Tegan turned his back on her and left with the rest of the soldiers.

CHAPTER EIGHTEEN

Mira wasn't sure if her message had sunk in, but she hoped that deep down, she'd been able to plant the seed of truth.

Lucian's weak groan brought her focus back to him. In the cramped cell there was hardly room to move, but Mira turned on the men, careful not to step on them, and looked with horror at her friend laying limply in George's arms. So many thoughts and feelings were swarming around inside of her. The sight of Lucian, pale and weak, lying in George's lap brought tears to her eyes. She couldn't even remember the last time she'd actually cried. "Will he be okay?" The question came out before she'd decided whether she wanted to know the answer.

"Yes." George held fast to Lucian's trembling body. "He's in shock, but he's healing."

"What?" Mira's heart skipped a beat.

"Natasha thought it would motivate you, so she stabbed him and left him here in the cell with us."

"She wanted me to turn him," Mira said. "That's all the Council has wanted since the moment I brought the humans to them. Well, she's not getting that from me, but what she will get is payment on the blood oath she gave regarding his safety."

"Yeah. Stryker said you didn't want him turned." George's calm tone was reassuring. "He'll be fine. He didn't bleed out too badly before I got to him. I've given him small sips here and there to heal, but he won't turn."

Relief sent more tears streaming down her face.

She knelt down and pulled Lucian into her lap. Brushing away the hair sticking to his forehead, she found his eyes. Half-closed and unfocused, she could see he was trying to fight the fatigue of blood loss. "Sorry," she whispered in his ear. "I never thought it would come to this."

"Guess I should have let you deal with Niko in the streets," Stryker said. He did not meet her eyes, hanging his head low with shame. "I had no idea this was their plan."

"No. You're right. They need to be dealt with in private. The humans, or what remains of them, don't need to see us all fighting amongst ourselves. They needed to see level heads and a willingness to discuss things. Not savagery!"

"I never thought them possible of such deceit." Stryker was beside himself with emotion. He looked as if he wanted to pummel the very ground to release his pent-up aggression. "They've gone mad with power. The Council has gone too far."

"The only thing we can do now is eliminate them. Stop the madness ourselves."

"But I thought you were done with all the killing and war." Stryker's tone lacked the sarcasm his words should have held.

A growl rumbled up Mira's throat as she looked down on Lucian's ghostly white face. The human was weak, but she could hear his heartbeat. He'd live. "Fighting is my lot in life, it seems." She'd make them pay first, and then eliminate them.

"Well, no one will be fighting in here," George pointed out.

"Then we'll get out." Mira turned and smiled.

"You performed one magic trick, escaping that first time… however will you manage it again?" George asked.

Stryker looked on at her with confusion.

"Five digits… when I was imprisoned here it was ten. Tegan is not so smart if he thinks I don't remember keytones. How many years have I been listening to them?" She smirked and reached her hand through the bars. The silver stung her skin, but she wasn't about to let that stop her. The keypad was awkwardly positioned. She had never tried to enter the keys herself. The tones she knew well enough, but the placement of the keys was difficult for her fingers to press. She hit a few buttons at random, noting the sounds and listening for a response to incorrect entries. She'd hoped for something, any indication, that an entry was accepted or rejected, but she heard nothing.

"Lucian… wake up." Mira bent down and gently shook him. "What can you tell me about the locks?"

He groaned, but his eyes refused to open.

"Five digits should be easy enough," she mumbled, trying to recall the tone she'd heard. "But if I enter it wrong, what will happen?" Reaching her hand through the bars again, she tried to duplicate the tone. Nothing. No soft click of the bars unlocking nor any harsh beeps of rejection. "Is there something else that I'm missing?"

George looked down at Lucian. His breathing was too shallow for consciousness. "He's probably going to be out for a while."

"Give him more blood!" Desperation sharpened her tone.

"I can't give him too much. You know what would happen."

George was right. Mira remembered the botched transformation she'd been a test subject on. The painful howls of the human they were experimenting on were almost too much to hear. She couldn't do that to Lucian. Too much blood at this point would poison his body rather than heal it.

She said a silent prayer to her gods and tried again. This time she felt around the keypad before pressing the buttons. Four rows of square keys, three keys across, except for the bottom row which only had two. But one was longer than the other. An enter key, maybe? Mira took a deep breath and tried the tones again, this time finishing off with the longer key.

The locks shifted, she heard the soft click she'd been longing to hear and the door slid open.

"Let me never doubt you again," George smiled.

"We need to get out of here and get reinforcements." Mira looked to Stryker. "Can I trust you?"

For a moment, he looked hurt, but he did not say anything to confirm it. She hadn't meant to insult him, but so many had betrayed her trust in the last two days, it was almost an involuntary question now. To his credit, Stryker simply nodded. "Lead the way."

"George, stay with Lucian and protect him. I'm putting an end to this bloody war!"

"Do what you have to do." George winked at Mira. "I'll take good care of him for you." Of that Mira had no doubt. She never needed to question George's loyalties.

CHAPTER NINETEEN

S he wished she had Lucian with her as she and Stryker made their way again through the maze of cells, corridors, and winding staircases. Even after their recent escape and rescue, she still found herself getting turned around at almost every corridor.

Stryker kept quiet as they ran. She wondered if she'd insulted him with her earlier question of trust.

She hadn't meant it. She did trust him. He'd become her friend. And maybe more than that… though she wasn't sure if she was ready to admit it.

"Sorry for what I said back there."

"No need to apologize. My people have wronged you just as much as the humans. I wouldn't trust me either."

"But I do," she said, and truly meant it. "I know you're trustworthy."

"I'm honored. I will not break that trust like my people have. I give you my blood oath on it."

Those Otherkin and their blood oaths! It was a dangerous thing to make one to Mira; she was not hesitant about collecting. Though there was no worry she'd have to do that with Stryker. "And you have mine." Before things got too touchy feely, Mira rounded a corner and finally found a doorway she recognized. "Now let's go take down the Council."

"Do you have a plan?" Stryker cautiously asked.

Through the doors, Mira recognized the smell of the arena. They had to be just below it, near the stables. All she needed to find now was the elevators to take her up to the Elite box.

"No." Not unless ripping a few throats out counts. "I'm winging it."

They entered the stables, and Mira walked straight to the weapons room. Normally it was guarded by handlers, but since they'd been taken out, the weapons supply was all hers to plunder. She grabbed an old favorite sword and pointed Stryker to the wall of weapons.

"Take what you need."

His eyes lit with childhood excitement at the sight of all the weapons. "I'm more of a hand to hand guy, but I won't say no to a few of these." He pulled a set of throwing knives from a shelf and pocketed them.

"Five Council members left, and two of us. Should be an easy fight." Stryker's tone was fairly calm, given what he was proposing.

Mira, however, burned with rage. Behind the weapons room was a door Mira had never ventured through. Given that it was used by the humans only, she expected more tunnels and mazes, but found something so much better. An elevator.

Luck was on their side for a change, and Mira felt a small bit of hope rising through the anger and rage as they made their way toward the elevators and up to the Elites' box.

Inside, the Council – what remained of them – would be sitting, enjoying the show as vampires were massacring humans in the arena below.

"I have you covered. Just point me at someone you want taken down." The humor behind his words failed to lighten her mood.

"Be prepared to kill. Unless you take issue with the death of your leaders."

"They ceased to be my leaders when they turned on me."

Confusion creased her brow.

"Mira, you're one of us. The fact that you were incarcerated for most of your immortal life does not change that fact. The Council swore to protect us. Burning with light weapons, caging behind metal bars, these are things that humans do. They've turned on you… and me. Now, their actions condemn us all. They're not my leaders anymore."

Sweet as his words were, Mira had no time for sentimentality. "Good. Then be prepared to remove them from power, by whatever means possible."

Rage overtook her desire for peace, and her mouth watered at the prospect of tasting more Otherkin blood.

Guards were posted at the entrance to the Elite box. Two of them, and from the sound of footsteps in the hall, there were another couple on patrol.

She sized up the stationary males. Not vampires by the looks of them; their skin was too dark. They might be shifters, ones who were out in the sun quite a bit, by the looks of it. Tanned skin, toned muscles. They'd be quick, and probably strong, but she doubted they would pose much of a threat to her.

"You know them?" she whispered to Stryker.

"Marrok and Cyphur. Hawk shifters. Niko's kin. They're fast and excellent with hand to hand combat. Watch the claws."

Her eyes darted to their hands. She should have noticed before — their nails were not only long, but also talon-like with a slight hook to them.

"I bet I'm faster. I have the one on the right; you take the left."

"Don't kill them. They're good guys. Just following orders." Stryker's tone was more concerned than she was comfortable with.

"No promises." She didn't wait for him to say another word. Darting across the hall, she was already heading toward her prey. Sliding into him like a ballplayer, she took the first soldier down before he had a chance to retaliate, but when he hit the ground, rather than slump to the floor, he rolled just out of her reach.

Impressed with his agility, Mira smiled as she dodged his claw-like nails. He swiped at her wildly as he backed toward the door.

Out of the corner of her eye, Mira saw the swift blur of Stryker tumbling with his solider.

She refocused on her quarry, meeting his piercing stare. Not smart enough to be afraid, the hawk shifter narrowed his eyes as if he could by shear will force her to surrender.

It took all her strength and resolve not to tear out his throat. Putting her supernatural speed to good use, she threw her shoulder into his chest, knocking the wind out of him, and then dragged his coughing body to the ground before mounting him and pinning his arms down.

"You're a good man from what I hear. I am not your ene-my… unless you make me so. Remember that when you wake up." She threw her head hard into his, knocking the soldier unconscious. Her own head throbbed from the blow, but not nearly as badly as the soldier's would when he woke. She listened for sound of his breathing before lifting herself up and turning toward Stryker. He was still wrestling with his soldier, neither one really looking like their heart was in the fight.

"There's no shame in yielding when the person you're fighting is on the right side of the war." Mira approached the pair and looked down at both. Stryker had gained the upper hand for a moment. On her approach, both men went still.

"I have orders." The soldier's words sounded rehearsed rather than from the heart.

"I'll give you better ones," Mira replied, and extended her hand.

"They'll have my head…"

"And I could have your neck. Either way, bad luck for you. But I'm not here for you. And I'm willing to bet you're not here out of choice."

"What would you have me do?"

"Go home."

The soldier looked perplexed.

"This war with the humans has to stop. And that will only happen when this madness stops. Go home, sleep with your wife, make lots of little hawk-shifter babies. Leave the fighting to me."

"But the Council…"

"Will have nothing more to say after I go in there." Mira's fangs practically hummed with anticipation as she imagined taking their blood and ending this new reign of terror.

He seemed to understand, taking her outstretched hand and allowing her to lift him up.

"For appearance's sake, I'd rather you knocked me out like Marrok."

Mira head-butted him before he could say another word. She managed to catch him before he completely crumpled to the ground, and left him in a heap.

Stryker cleared his throat. When Mira looked at him, he was pointing toward the sound of footsteps heading their way. "Probably two more. Do you want me to wait here for them?"

"I might need you inside with me."

"Then let's get moving. I'm sure the Council already knows you're out here."

"I'm sure Natasha and Michael do, at the very least. They're probably listening to this conversation through the door as we speak." Mira threw her shoulder into the door, bursting it open.

CHAPTER TWENTY

"**G**uards!" **Natasha shrieked** as Mira stepped through the shattered door.

A hand appeared in front of Mira's face. On instinct, she grabbed and pulled its owner down and threw her free elbow hard between the soldier's shoulder blades. Before he crumpled, she fisted a hand into his hair and yanked his head up. "Stop wasting others' lives and deal with me directly." She looked into the frightened soldier's eyes. "You don't want to fight me, do you?"

The soldier did not respond verbally, but his eyes screamed, "No!"

She threw him down, hoping he'd be smart enough to stay there.

Two other soldiers in the room halted in their tracks. Smart, Mira thought. Her reputation had its perks. No one wanted to fight with her.

"You'll deal with me one on one, Natasha." Mira fisted her hands, readying herself to fight. "I've come to collect on your blood oath."

Natasha's eye twitched ever so slightly. There was fear there that she did not want to admit.

"And when I am done with her," Mira said, "I will deal with the rest of you." She purposely made eye contact with the remaining members of the Council.

"Now, let's not be too hasty." Michael held his hands up in surrender, but took a step toward Mira.

"The time for talk is over. You've done nothing but lie and plot this war, using me and my people as chess pieces to your end."

"Wars have casualties…" Michael continued to slowly step closer.

"You're about to learn that firsthand." From the corner of her eye, she caught a shadow move on the wall. Michael's movements had only been a distraction, and Niko was suddenly at her side, arms raised with a table knife held like a dagger. She tilted backwards away from his swing and caught his hand, turning it on his own body, plunging the knife deep into his chest. She dropped him and returned her focus to Michael.

"Take Natasha," Mira ordered to Stryker. She took no time in lunging toward Michael.

Years of inactivity had not dulled his reflexes. Still, other than brute strength, he was not skilled in the art of combat. She had him pinned to the ground in moments.

"Please…" Michael pleaded.

"Say something stupid. Give me more lies to rally to your cause and continue this war." She spat in his face.

"I only did what I thought was right to save our people. You don't know what it was like when the humans took over."

"That doesn't matter. I will not see the other side repeat the same mistake." She dove at his neck, sinking her teeth in deep. She shouldn't, but she couldn't help herself. Fresh blood called to her, and she gulped down what she could in the few seconds she had before ripping Michael's throat out. His blood pooled around them, staining everything in its path. Mesmerized, she watched it for a moment before finishing Michael off, removing his head like she'd done so many times in the arena.

She must have looked crazed, or maybe it was the act of ripping another being's head from his body that gave the others the true sense of what she'd had to do as a gladiator, but after that the room fell silent.

"Yes, this is what happens to losers in the arena…" She spat a chunk of flesh on the ground and stood, meeting the eyes of all in the room in turn.

Roseanna, Natasha, and Katerina were all that remained. Male or female, it didn't matter to Mira – she was prepared to kill.

Natasha stopped struggling in Stryker's grip. "Release me," she demanded.

"You promised no harm would come to my friend. You gave your blood oath to it. Now I collect payment. " Mira turned on Natasha with all the quickness of her race. "Let this be a lesson to those of you that remain." She snapped Natasha's neck, and then took a deep breath before fully removing her head. The room was soaked in blood, and Mira's face was drenched with it when she turned around to face the last two on the Council.

"You." She pointed to Katerina.

The redheaded woman, despite the fear in her eyes, stood calmly and stepped up to Mira. "Do what you must."

She hadn't expected that.

A quick glance at Stryker stayed Mira's hand. "Are you planning to cross me?" she asked the shifter woman.

"It was never my intention. I am only here to speak for my people's needs." Katerina's voice waivered some. Genuine fear. But Mira also sensed truth.

"You will step down. Stryker will speak for your people from now on."

"As you wish." Katerina nodded, taking her eyes off of Mira for the briefest of moments to look at Stryker. "I will follow you both."

That went much more easily than she'd anticipated. Though she sensed the shifter was honest, she'd keep an eye on her in the future.

"And Roseanna…" Mira licked her fangs clean as she addressed the final member of the council.

"If it's all the same, I do not want to die." She held her hands up in surrender.

Roseanna had been unusually quiet in all her dealings with Mira. Each time she had appeared to simply agree with her male counterpart, Alec. Mira wondered how much of that might have been controlled by the former Otherkin leader. Just as with Katerina, Mira sensed honesty in this Otherkin woman. For the moment, she'd let her live too. "Then don't give me a reason to kill you."

"Understood." Roseanna sighed with relief and lowered her hands. "What do you want me to do?"

"Nothing for the moment. But you will answer to my every order while we deal with the fallout."

"Understood."

Mira looked to Stryker. "Stay here with them. I have to end these games."

CHAPTER TWENTY-ONE

"**S top this madness!**" Mira shouted as she stormed into the arena.

Tegan turned back from his prey, the shivering blob of frightened human that had once been the proud and cocky Magistrate. His face had been beaten so bloody he was hardly recognizable.

The crowd above, a mix of human and Otherkin, called out from the stands. Mira could hardly tell if they were for or against her interruption. She looked to the large screen and saw herself magnified as she had so many times in the past in its HD display.

"This is not the way," she shouted again.

"Kill him." A loud voice rang out through the crowd.

Mira could not tell who had said it, but she looked up again and addressed the masses. "What will killing him solve? Will it get back any of the others who died under his rule?"

"He deserves death. Make him pay for his crimes." More shouts, more angered cries.

"Death is too quick a payment. Too easy. He's lived his life on the deaths of others. Wouldn't it be more just to make him work towards the opposite?" Mira shouted up to the crowd. "Make him a servant of peace."

Tegan stood from his attack stance and turned to fully face Mira. "Give it up. This one is a lost cause. The people need to see him pay. And I need my revenge."

"Don't you see? You're just continuing the cycle. After his death, who next? There are so many who have been responsible for our suffering over the years. We could end them all and feel vindicated, but what trail of hatred would we leave behind? Friends and family of those we killed would eventually want revenge. The cycle will never end unless we stop it ourselves. Yes, they're guilty of horrible atrocities. Yes, they have hurt our kind for generations. Yes, they deserve some retribution. But let that be justified. Let it be working toward peace and an end to hostility. Let that be their punishment rather than ending their existence."

"Kill me." The Magistrate struggled to his feet. "I'll never allow this peace. You and all of your kind are abominations. Monsters!"

"You see, he deserves to die. He can be our example," Tegan said with an evil smirk.

Mira shook her head. "Don't you see? That's exactly what he wants. You kill him and his suffering ends. And, you prove to all the rest of the humans that we only know how to deal with things by dishing out death."

"Do it. You know you want to." The Magistrate limped forward and threw himself onto Tegan. "Smell that blood. You know you can't resist."

Tegan closed his eyes and inhaled slowly. "We can make examples of others. This one is mine."

"Over my dead body," Mira said, and lunged toward Tegan. She ripped the Magistrate from his grasp and tossed him to the ground. "Don't make me fight you, Tegan." Mira warned.

"I don't want to fight you. I want to kill him." A feral edge took over Tegan's voice.

Mira crouched low, pulling her sword from its sheath, ready to fight if necessary.

The crowd roared with excitement above.

"You see? All they want is blood," Tegan said, his voice dripping with "I told you so.".

"Because that's all they have been told to want." Mira replied. "You know you cannot win, Tegan. I'm stronger and a better fighter. We've danced around this arena many times. Stand down."

Tegan let out a growl of frustration that could rival that from any feral wolf, but afterwards, he relaxed his posture and lowered his fists. "I hope you're right about this. Because I have my doubts."

Mira rose to stand, dropped her sword to the ground, and extended her hand in friendship. "I have my doubts too, but we have to at least try."

Tegan took it and nodded. "You've always had my respect as a fighter, but now I see in you the makings of a wise leader, too."

"And I always thought you hated me." Though she and he had always been enemies on some level, Mira had also respected him for his abilities. To hear that the feeling was mutual was a compliment of the highest regard.

"No one likes being beaten by a girl," Tegan said under his breath.

The crowd above displayed a mix of emotions – some people cheered, some shouted. Mira noted a few fights breaking out in the stands.

"We've got our work cut out for us," she said to herself, though she knew Tegan could hear. Before she could call out for assistance in the stands, she saw members of the wolf pack already heading to break up some of the fights.

"Mira, look out!" someone called from the stands.

Mira turned in time to see the Magistrate lunging toward her with the sword in his hand.

"This is what I think of your peace," he shouted.

Mira sidestepped out of his clumsy path. The Magistrate went down hard on to the ground, impaling himself on the sword.

"So much for leaving him alive," Tegan smirked.

"At least we didn't kill him," Mira said.

"There's still time…"

Mira nodded at Tegan's unspoken suggestion. Poetic justice for the man responsible for so many of her kind's death. The same fate she'd condemned Olivia to as well.

Tegan bend down low and pulled the flabby dying man up into his arms. Like a viper, he went for the carotid artery, severing it with his teeth. Minutes went by in slow motion. Every second of what was happening was being played out on the big screen. Humans had always wondered how it was done – and now they would witness it firsthand. Tegan drank his fill and then ripped open his own flesh, biting into his wrist, and fed the Magistrate his blood.

Unresponsive at first, Mira wondered if Tegan had waited too long, let too much blood be lost; but then the Magistrate swallowed. His heart picked up beating again. He was turning.

Mira looked up and addressed the crowd. "Bad blood has torn our people apart for centuries. Rumors, prejudices, and unnecessary fear have all fed into our races this outright hatred of one another." Silence filled the arena. She knew she had their attention. Never really being good with words, however, she felt at a loss as to what to say. "We are all creatures of this earth. Each and every one of us deserves to be here."

To her left, the door to the stables opened. George entered the arena, carrying Lucian in his arms. Worry stole Mira's attention. Was he still alive? She dared not move or speak until she heard the beating of his heart. Lucian was awake, but still very weak. He smiled, seeing Mira. "Go on. Tell them. You can do it."

His encouragement gave her confidence.

"From this moment on, we must make a change." She addressed the crowd again. "We must learn to co-exist."

Murmurs of agreement came from the crowd above, but no one was brave enough to say it outright.

Mira hoped they were really listening. Taking in her message. Seeing the truth.

Lucian reached out and put a hand on Mira's shoulder. For the first time, she didn't feel the need to shrug it away. She turned and smiled at her friend.

"If we cannot learn to live with each other, the cycle of violence and death will continue. You'll be condemning your children and your children's children to a future of bloodshed."

She hadn't heard the doors open but Stryker, Katerina, and Roseanna strolled into the arena with them. They joined Mira in the center. She was never more grateful for the show of solidarity, something she'd honestly never expected to see happen.

"The reign of terror is over." She looked up to the crowd again. "We all stand here before you: Human, Otherkin, Shifter, and Vampire. United by a common goal... peace. Will you join us in this cause?"

Mira looked up to the stands, watching the people sitting there. All that remained of this human city were women, children, and a few old men, incapable of fighting, but hardly any others. The rest of the spectators were Otherkin.

Long silent moments went by before one person stood and began clapping. Then two, and finally one by one the arena grew to a roar of applause.

Mira let out a long sigh of relief.

"You know, pretty speeches aside, there's a lot of work to be done to realize your dream of peace," Lucian said.

He was right, and that worried her. What had she taken on?

Before the worry could take root in Mira's mind, Stryker hugged her from behind. "Lucky she has us to help her."

Normally she'd have shied away or reacted violently to such an intimate gesture, but at that moment, she needed his arms around her. He made her feel whole, complete. More than just a friend, he'd become a companion to her during their short time together.

Mira turned to face Stryker, smiling as she saw the shock in his amber eyes. "I do feel lucky." She planted a quick peck on his nose before squirreling out of his grip.

Stryker's jaw almost hit the floor, and Mira wasn't the only one who caught the shocked expression.

George snorted, almost dropping Lucian on the ground. "Told you she liked you," he snickered.

Mira would neither confirm nor deny that, but she smiled all the same.

Lucian wasn't smiling, but he didn't appear as surprised as the rest. He nodded at Mira and whispered, "Somewhere deep down, I knew it could never be me."

"You and I have a different bond," she replied just as quietly. "But no less strong."

She turned from Lucian, meeting each pair of eyes surrounding her. "And we all need to be strong in the coming days. It will be our bond of friendship that sets the tone for what is to come."

Seeing everyone there, in the arena with her, Mira felt a weight lift from her shoulders. They'd been through hell, but here they stood, former enemies, smiling and standing together as one. A shining example of what could be.

"All I have ever wanted was an end to the fighting." Mira continued. "Hopefully with your help, as representatives of each of your kind, we can truly create peace for all of our people."

"To peace!" Stryker called out and held his arm up in the air.

"Peace," the others chanted.

Above them, the chant echoed in the stands. "Peace!"

Mira knew it would be tough to hold on to, but for the moment, she'd finally found it.

TRANSITION

Chronicles of the Uprising: 4
Sample Chapter 1

Thousands of stars twinkled overhead as Mira sat on the balcony of her new suite in the capital building of New Haven. Not long before, this city had been a place feared by vampires for its cruelty. Now it had become the center for all vampire refugees around the continent. And Mira had become the unlikely leader and hero of her kind.

The suite she called her own was comfortable and filled with every amenity she could have ever wished for, but Mira was only truly content when sitting on its balcony with the simple patio furniture, staring up at the night sky. She'd stay there all night if people would let her. She'd found her way out of the prison, and earned the respect of the Otherkin, but freedom had not truly been gifted to her. She'd traded the weight of silver shackles for ones heavy with respect and leadership. And though she craved the simple life, it was not meant to be hers, at least for this moment.

"Did you want to inspect the demolition?" Stryker's voice pierced the quiet serenity of the patio.

Mira had been so deep in thought that the sound of his voice startled her, almost making her jump in her seat. "What?"

She turned to her mate, meeting his amber eyes with annoyance at being interrupted during the few minutes she'd found to escape.

The werewolf did not back down from Mira's heated glare. He matched her aggression with his own. "Don't give me that look. You're a figurehead around here, and you have duties to attend to."

They could play this dominance game all night. Both alphas in their own right, Mira and Stryker were evenly matched fighters – though she, as a vampire, had a little more advantage when it was night. But this was not an issue for them to fight about. He was right, of course; she had her duties to the city now, though this was not the part she'd ever planned to play. She was no leader. All she had ever wanted was to find peace. Fate, it seemed, had dealt her an entirely different hand, and she had a particular distaste for politics and management.

With a heavy sigh, Mira stood and walked toward Stryker, stopping just out of arm's reach. "I just needed some air after hearing the report about the southern cities. I'm ready to go back to work. What is it you need me to see?"

"The southern cities can wait. I have something a little more interesting for you."

In the few months they had known each other, he'd learned to love her for her quirks, the way she avoided physical contact, and how closely she guarded her inner feelings. Though she stood just out of his reach, he stepped in and grasped her hand, daring her to pull away. Sometimes she did; this time, however, she held tightly. "The wrecking crew is down in the stables, dismantling them. I thought it might be therapeutic for you."

Stryker stood a head taller than Mira, and she was forced to crane her neck to look at him. So unlike other men she knew, he was gentle, though just as deadly a warrior as she. He considered her thoughts and feelings when she didn't even know she had them. Even now he'd found a way to soothe away the anxiety she didn't even realize she was feeling. She stood on tiptoe and quickly pecked him on the cheek. "Thank you."

Gestures like this were few and far between, and Stryker knew better than to make a big deal of them. Mira was slowly coming around and letting her guard down. To call her out on it would only slam the doors shut on any progress she'd made.

"Walk with me," Stryker said, and before she could answer, he pulled her along with him.

Mira hadn't been down there in weeks. In truth, she avoided that building at all costs. Too many painful memories; too much blood on her hands. She'd ordered it demolished, and a park with grass and trees was meant to replace what had once stood as a place of death.

"Promise me that after we're done looking, we can take the rest of the night off."

"You know I can't promise that, but let's try." He squeezed her hand, a gesture that shouldn't have bothered her, but Mira had to fight the urge to let go and back away.

She'd been working so hard on being comfortable with touching, especially with Stryker. He was her mate, after all. She had chosen to be with him, though her own issues prevented her from completely letting him in yet. But she was making progress. A kiss here, a hug there, and even a few late night cuddles. Things like that seemed so foreign to her, though they had not always been so. Years as a gladiator, only coming into contact with others to kill them, had a way of hardening a person, and had trained Mira to avoid contact at all costs. Stryker was like her: a warrior, but a different sort. One who embraced touch and closeness, and only fought when he had to. A good model for her, and damn near the perfect kind of mate. He balanced her and calmed her anxieties, but was also able to defend when a wild punch came from her instinct to fight.

Still holding tightly, despite her desire to let go, Mira and Stryker walked hand in hand down through the capitol building's residence corridors and into the lower levels where the private tunnels would take them to the heart of the prison Mira had once been forced to call home.

Her heightened senses picked up on the stench of death as they walked. Old blood – the smell of it had long since embedded itself into the very heart of the building. No cleaners on earth could wash away the years of murder these walls contained. It was for this reason alone Mira had ordered its destruction. There was no way the arena, and the prison underneath, could stand while she and her people worked toward peace among the species.

Anxiety sent her heart racing as they entered the tunnels down to the stables and the lower prison where she'd once been forced to live and wait for her time in the arena. Even now, silent as the place was, Mira could hear the cries. So many vampires had come through these rooms, and so few had actually made it out.

Stryker, sensing her unease, released her hand and let her walk on alone. Crowding her would only have the opposite effect. She needed her space to work through her demons.

"Are you ready to see the best part?" he asked, as they entered the prison.

Mira did not answer. She just walked on, through the doors and into a room of frenzied construction workers. Jackhammers, chisels, wheelbarrows scraping the ground, rock being broken and moved – the noise alone was deafening, but at the same time, a beautiful symphony of destruction.

Mira smiled at seeing the wreckage of UV lights dismantled, never to burn her eyes again. Stryker was right; this was exactly what she had needed to see. Already the tightening of her chest was lessening, and even though the stench of death lingered in the air, she found it easier to breathe here now.

They passed by what had once been her cell. The demolition crew had already begun work dismantling bars and jackhammering the floor. Workers were taking out huge chunks of the ground piece by piece, as the floor was disassembled, Mira caught sight of something: a book buried among the rubble.

"Hold on," she yelled to the worker who was jackhammering away. He didn't hear, but as she approached he stopped and angrily glared at her. Mira bypassed the stunned worker, ignoring his annoyed huff, and walked into the cell to retrieve it. Though it was dusty, with a cracking spine, Mira nevertheless recognized it instantly. "I thought I had lost you forever."

"What it is?" Stryker asked.

Years had stolen many things from Mira. She'd come to understand that nothing in this place was permanent. When the journal had disappeared, she'd just assumed that was the end of it; but now, holding it in her hands, it was as if she'd taken back a small bit of her life. "This is my journal." Mira beamed as she opened the old leather notebook and thumbed through the pages. "I wrote in it when I first came to this prison. It kept me sane for a short while."

"Somehow I don't see you as the journaling type." Stryker laughed and instantly jumped backwards, as if expecting Mira to smack him.

To do that, though, she'd have had to take a hand off the journal, and now that she had it in her grasp again, she wasn't letting go. "You'd be surprised how different I was back then."

"Wait a second. How the hell did you write a journal? Where did you get it?"

"I found it. After I'd been locked in here, I tore apart my cell. Not the smartest move, but I was angry, and destruction was my only outlet."

"That doesn't surprise me. You're still a bit destructive."

She ignored his little jab. "Whoever had this cell before me must have had it. Probably a gift from their patron or something. It really didn't matter. I ripped out their pages and filled in my own."

"And how did you manage to keep it?"

"I didn't. I lost it. Somehow it must have fallen through the cracks between the cell's UV light panels and gotten lodged in the floor. I haven't seen this book since the very beginning of my incarceration."

"May I?" Stryker asked.

Mira wasn't ready to hand it over, even to Stryker. "How about we go back and read it together?"

"Together? That sounds good. Are you sure you want to share it all?" Stryker's tone was unusually cautious.

"I think you'll gain some interesting perspective from it." Mira laughed. "I was a stupid kid with a mind for adventure, and I got exactly what I was after."

"Of that I have no doubt. I'm guessing you were always mouthy and feisty, too. I don't think that came from being imprisoned."

"Some of it, no. I owe a lot of that to my mentors."

"You had mentors?"

"They didn't know it, but yes. If not for the people who brought me here, I'd have never grown the balls to survive."

"Well, you've piqued my interest."

"I'll share, but be warned – this is not a happy tale."

Stryker's eyebrow lifted in curiosity.

Mira leading the way this time, they retreated back to the balcony in Mira's suite, taking places around her small café table as she opened her journal and prepared to read.

The words she'd written so long ago seemed almost foreign, now that she was looking at them again. Their memory though came flooding back as she began to read aloud.

OTHER TITLES BY KATIE SALIDAS

The Immortalis Series:

Becoming a vampire is easy. Living with the condition... that's the hard part. Join Alyssa as she stumbles through the world of the "Unnatural."

Book 1: Immortalis Carpe Noctem - Newbie vampire Alyssa never asked for this life, but now it's all she has. Rescued from death by Lysander, the aloof and sexy leader of the Peregrinus vampire clan, she's barely cut her teeth before she becomes a target. Kallisto, an ancient and vindictive vampire queen – and Lysander's old mate - wants nothing less than final death for her former lover and his new toy. She's not above letting the Acta Sanctorum, and its greatest vampire hunter, Santino, know exactly where the clan can be found. With no time to mourn her old life, Alyssa's survival depends on her new family. She will have to stand alongside Lysander and fight against two enemies who will stop at nothing to destroy them.

Book 2: Hunters & Prey - Rule number one: humans and vampires don't co-exist. One is the hunter and one is the prey. Simple, right? Not for newly-turned vampire Alyssa. A surprise confrontation with Santino Vitale, the Acta Sanctorum's most fearsome hunter, sends her fleeing back to the world she once knew, and Fallon, the human friend she's missed more than anything. Now she has some explaining to do. However, that will have to wait. With the Acta Sanctorum hot on their heels, staying alive is more important than educating a human on the finer points of bloodlust.

Book 3: Pandora's Box - After a few months as a vampire, Alyssa thought she'd learned all she needed to know about the supernatural world. But her confidence is shattered by the delivery of a mysterious package - a Pandora's Box. Seemingly innocuous, the box is in reality an ancient prison, generated by a magic more powerful than anyone in her clan has ever known. But what manner of evil could need such force to contain it? When the box is opened, the sinister creature within is released, and only supernatural blood will satiate its thirst. The clan soon learns how it feels when the hunter becomes the hunted.

Book 4: Soulstone - It's a desperate time for rookie vampire Alyssa, and her sanity is hanging by a slender thread. Her clan is still reeling from the monumental battle with Aniketos; a battle that claimed the body of Lysander, her sire and lover, and trapped his spirit in a mysterious crystal. A Soulstone. Unfortunately, no amount of magic has been able to release Lysander's spirit, and the stone is starting to fade. Weeks of effort have proved futile. Her clan, the Peregrinus, have all but given up hope. Only Alyssa still believes her lover can be released. In despair, Alyssa begs the help of the local witch coven, and unwittingly exposes the supernaturals of Boston to unwanted attention from the Acta Sanctorum. The Saints converge on the city and begin their cleansing crusade to rid the world of all things "Unnatural." In the middle of an all-out war, but no closer to a solution to the dying stone, Alyssa is left with an unenviable choice: save her mate, or save her clan.

Book 5: Moonlight
Good girls don't wear fur, or fight over men, and they certainly don't run around naked, howling at the moon. But then, no-one ever called Fallon a good girl. As a human *unofficially* mated to an Alpha werewolf, Fallon is being pressured to "become"...or be gone. Her mate Aiden, the interim leader of the Olde Town Pack, is in a position that demands he either choose a wolf mate...or leave the pack forever. No matter how hot the sex

with Fallon is, he can't ignore centuries of tradition. Become a wolf or not. If only the choice were that simple. Fallon's options are further clouded by the overt presence of other females desperate to be the Alpha's mate. And when these bitches get serious, it's not just claws that come out. If Fallon wants to keep her man and take the title she'll have to exert a little dominance of her own.

Book 6: Dark Salvation

A gathering storm of violence is on the horizon. Whispered threats of the Acta Sanctorum's return have the supernatural world abuzz. Only recently aware of the other world hidden behind our own, Kitara Vanders has barely scratched the surface of what being supernatural truly means. A special woman in her own right, she possesses unique telepathic abilities, gifts that have recently come under the scrutiny of the Acta Sanctorum, a fanatical organization whose mission is to cleanse the world of anything supernatural. Targeted, and marked for death, Kitara's only hope lies with the lethally seductive yet emotionally scarred warrior, Nicholas.

Knowing full well the atrocities the Acta Sanctorum is capable of, Nicholas is all too eager for the battle to begin. Fueled by pain and rage from the loss of his mate, he's itching for a fight, but one thing stands in his way, Kitara: a beautiful dark-haired woman with unique psychic abilities and an unusual link to the Saints. Despite his resolve to remain focused on his mission, a purely physical relationship binds them together in a way neither of them expected. And when her life hangs in the balance, Nicholas finds his own is teetering on the edge too.

ABOUT THE AUTHOR

Katie Salidas is a Super Woman! Endowed with special powers and abilities, beyond those of mortal women, She can get the munchkin off to gymnastics, cheerleading, Girl Scouts, and swim lessons. She can put hot food on the table for dinner while assisting with homework, baths, and bedtime... And, She still finds the time to keep the hubby happy (nudge nudge wink wink). She can do all of this and still have time to write.

And if you can believe all of those lies, there is some beautiful swamp land in Florida for sale...

Katie Salidas resides in Las Vegas, Nevada. Mother, wife, and author, she does try to do it all, often causing sleep deprivation and many nights passed out at the computer. Writing books is her passion, and she hopes that her passion will bring you hours of entertainment.

Find Katie Salidas online at:

http://www.katiesalidas.com/

Facebook
http://www.facebook.com/pages/Katie-Salidas-Author/214780936916

LinkedIn
http://www.linkedin.com/profile?viewProfile=&key=58814031&trk=tab_pro

Twitter
http://twitter.com/QuixoticKatie